The Great Thirst

The Great Thirst
JENNY SEED

BRADBURY PRESS · SCARSDALE, N.Y.

Library of Congress Catalog Card Number: 73-80198.
ISBN 0-87888-058-5.
Manufactured in Great Britain.
First American Edition published by Bradbury Press, Inc., 1973.

The text of this book is set in 11 pt. Baskerville.

Printed in Great Britain by
Cox and Wyman Ltd.,
London, Fakenham and Reading

To my sister, Jewel Huebsch

Author's Note

The country known today as South-West Africa occupies a vast territory, but it is, for the most part, a land of desert and drought, a place of stunted scrub and dry river beds that lie like pale scars across the sun-scorched earth. Bordered on the west by the shifting orange sands of the great Namib and on the east by the waterless tracts of the Kalahari, it is a cruel land. Yet in its magnitude and silence and the grey and gold of its endless plains it has a unique and fascinating beauty.

The early history of South-West Africa has been lost in time. It is known only that in the beginning were the primitive hunters and collectors of roots, the Bushmen. Then down from the north-east came the fierce agile little yellow-brown Hottentots with their small black-skinned servants, the Bergdama or Mountain People, and their long-horned cattle and fat-tailed sheep, and easily overcame the original inhabitants. They were the conquerors and masters and they called themselves triumphantly Khoi-khoi, The Men of Men, The Superior People.

Some of these victorious Hottentot tribes settled in scattered family clans around the waterholes and fountains of the southern plains of the south west and became known as the Nama peoples. The others trekked on over the Orange River, the Great River as it was called, and made their homes in what later became first the Dutch, then the British colony of the Cape.

But no sooner were they settled than another great migration was taking place. The Hereros, or Cattle People, with their broad-bladed spears and enormous herds were moving slowly southward in search of pasturage and water. Ebony-skinned, aristocratic-featured, and half as tall again as the little Namas, the Hereros are believed to have made their homes on

7

the northern savannahs of the country in the first half of the eighteenth century.

It was only a matter of time before these Cattle People, their advance accelerated by the great droughts of the 1820's, reached the central plateau which had long been the grazing lands of the Nama tribes, and came into conflict with the Men of Men.

The little Hottentots were no match for the tall powerful Hereros and may easily have experienced the same fate as the Bushmen before them except that at about this time an event occurred which changed the whole course of South-West African history.

A man named Jonker Afrikaner crossed the Orange River and entered Namaland. Small, shrewd and energetic, he was the chief of one of the old Hottentot tribes which had migrated farther south and which, driven from their grazing and hunting lands by the expanding Cape Colony, were looking for new homes among their Nama kinsmen. But these strangers were no ordinary Hottentots. They had absorbed white culture during their stay in the Cape. They rode on horses and carried firearms and their leader, Jonker Afrikaner, or Haramub as his people called him, was a man to be reckoned with. Historians have called him The Napoleon of the South, The Lion of Africa. When he spoke with his guns his voice was like the roar of a wild beast and all people trembled.

This then is the setting for *The Great Thirst*. It is the story of Garib, a Nama boy, who became entangled with Jonker Afrikaner and also with the white missionaries of various denominations who came to South-West Africa.

For the rest, the information used was found in records left by the early explorers, traders and missionaries who visited the country during this historic period, and, owing to the many clicks in the Hottentot language, the spelling of some of the names is, necessarily, only approximate.

And as for the people in the story, the boy Garib never existed in history, but Kahitjene, his mortal Herero foe and greatest of the Cattle Kings, did. So did Tjamuaha and his son Maherero, who afterwards became the first true paramount chief of the Herero nation, and so, of course, did Jonker Afrikaner, that "very bad man", who was condemned for his misdeeds to be buried in unhallowed ground and whose grave, incorporated at a later date in the new church lands in Okahandja, is a recently-declared national monument.

The Great Thirst

Principal Characters

of the Nama Peoples

"The Men of Men"
  Games, the queen
  Garib, a boy and then a man
  Arub the Hunter, his father
  Arub the Big One, Garib's uncle and chief of the
    clan
  Tomarib, counsellor and advisor to the chief
  Fast Foot, a hunter and a teacher to Garib
  Oasib, senior chief of the Nama nation after Games'
    death

"Warlike People"

  Haramub, also called Jonker Afrikaner
  Hendrik
  The Kaptein (Pieter) } two of Haramub's men
  Christian, Haramub's son

of the Cattle People

  Kahitjene, the Cattle King
  Tjamuaha, a chief } for a time allies of Haramub's
  Kamoja, a village chief
  Maherero, Tjamuaha's son

11

Prologue

In the Great Place of Games, queen of the largest tribe of the Nama nation, the doctor of the spirits raised the carved wooden pail in his arms and poured the white milk into the fire. It hissed and sighed as it fell into the hungry flames and an answering sigh rose from the throng of men standing behind him as they watched the ash-blackened liquid streaming down into the trench that had been dug to the side of the dancing area. The smoke rose up into the pale dusty sky and the sun's rays, filtering through the haze, bathed the whole scene in a golden light.

Dropping the pail, the doctor of the spirits lifted his knotted old arms above his head, and while he stood thus as if pleading with the heavens, more and yet more milk was thrown into the spluttering fire until the flames were at last extinguished and the liquid flowed like the running of rivers after the rains and the choking smoke billowed up like the great white thunder clouds before the storm.

"O Tsui-Goab!" he shouted.
Father of our Fathers!
Our Father!
Let the thunder clouds stream!
Let our flocks live!
Let us also live, O Father!
We are so weak,
From thirst,
From hunger:
Let us eat veld foods.
Art thou not our Father,
Father of our Fathers,
Thou Tsui-Goab?

We praise thee!
We bless thee!
Thou Father of our Fathers,
Thou, our Lord,
Thou, Tsui-Goab!

At the sound of his voice the men began to gather in a circle for the dance and the women, throwing off their sheepskin cloaks, moved forward, and a boy who was too young yet to leave women's company or to dance, jerked his thin knees close up under his chin in his excitement as he squatted beside his grandmother near the huts that surrounded the dancing field.

"Eisey!" he whispered under his breath, his small triangular face alive with eagerness and expectation. This was not the first time he had sat in the Great Place or watched the ceremony for the making of rain. He had travelled before with his father and the people of his clan from their distant home when the drought lay upon the land and the message had reached them that all men must gather at the house of the queen to pray and sacrifice so that the rain might fall in due season. But he could not clearly remember those other occasions. Now, after seven summers since his birth, it seemed his eyes were old enough to understand.

At that moment the leader of the flutes blew on his reed pipe. He blew strongly, his head bent forwards on to his bare chest and his feet beginning to stamp in the sand, and the other players in the ring in the centre of the dancing space joined in, each blowing his single note in time to the stamping of the leader so that the pipes, all blowing together, made sweet shrill music.

Then the dancing men took up the rhythm and the women sprang forward, clapping their hands before their faces, and ran round the men, their soft leather skirts swaying and the rings of hard hide round their legs and the ostrich shell beads round their necks rattling against each other as they too twisted and leapt and beat their heels upon the ground.

The people danced and sang, repeating the prayer over and over again and the small boy, wriggling and squirming with eagerness, moved farther away from his grandmother in his effort to see more clearly through the clouds of dust the dancers were kicking up. It was not the prayer that excited him, though, as always, it had sent a thrill of uneasiness through

14

him like the echo of some ancient fear. Even the men, he knew, thought little of the words they were singing, for on the long journey to the Great Place they had spoken of nothing but the feasting and festivities that were to follow.

No, it was the sight of the crowds that excited the boy. He could not remember seeing so many people together before. And more than this, though the faces that passed him were mostly the faces of strangers, he knew that among these dancers, half-hidden by the dust, were all the great men of the nation, men whom he had heard praised in song: rich headmen who owned many sheep and cattle, men who were quick and strong in the wrestling match, great hunters, and praised warriors who were masters of the bow and had proved their courage in battle with other quarrelling Nama tribes or against the cunning little Bushmen.

"Eisey!" he murmured again, and suddenly his eagerness would allow him to remain sitting no longer. Turning swiftly, he darted between the legs of some old men who were standing behind him and came out against the huts. He paused for a moment, his heart beating quickly with excitement at his own daring and also a little with fear for he had never been alone in a strange place before.

Running lightly around the ring of huts he stopped and, standing on tip-toe, strained to see over the shoulders of the people in front, but they were too tall and he could still see nothing.

Then as he moved impatiently his leg bumped against something hard. He glanced down in surprise. It was a large waterpot outside the entrance of one of the huts. He looked inside and saw that it was empty. Steadying the jar with his hands, he climbed on to it and stood balanced with his feet planted firmly on either side of its broad rim.

Ai! Now he could see above the dust. Was that the queen herself sitting on the carved wooden stool with a servant holding a sunshade of ostrich feathers over her head?

In his eagerness the boy had leant too far forward. The waterpot tilted and before he could think what was happening he was lying on his stomach with his face half buried in the soft dust outside the low entrance.

He gasped. Tears welled up in his eyes but he forced them back. He was determined not to cry. Roughly he rubbed the sand away and began to get up, then stopped in fright. A thin, reedy voice was speaking to him from within the hut.

"Who is there?" it said. "I think it is a child. Come here and let me see you, child!"

The boy's heart beat fast. He did not wish to enter a strange house but he dared not disobey a voice that spoke at the Great Place of the queen. Fearfully he crawled in through the low opening.

It was as if he had been swallowed up into the earth. He was blinded by the sudden darkness, then in the lessening gloom he saw the form of a man, half lying, half sitting, on a sheepskin bed in a hollow in the mud floor.

The boy crept towards the figure and knelt down.

"Ah!" A soft chuckle came from the pile of skin blankets. "Do not be afraid, child."

Quickly and shyly the boy looked up. He stared at the man, hardly believing at first that it could be a man, so wrinkled and lined was the old face peering towards him. And not only was the face as shrunken as a raisin that had been left too long in the sun, but the skin of the man's body, his neck and chest and even his arms, hung in great loose folds like an empty leather bag. And as he chuckled, a hand that was like a claw reached out, groping in the air as if seeking to find where the boy sat.

It was only then that the boy noticed the old man's eyes. Almost hidden though they were in the folds of skin, he could see that they were strange. A dull whitish film was stretched across them. The boy had seen this before in an old woman's eyes and he had been told that she was blind. But the man had said, "Let me see you."

The boy tried to draw back in fright but he was too late. The hand found his arm and caught hold of it.

"Who are you?" the old man asked, the wrinkles and lines forming themselves into a smile.

The boy was silent for a moment, too afraid to speak. Then he lifted his chin and said bravely, "I am Garib and my Great Name, my family name which shall be mine when I am made a man, is Arub. My father is Arub the Hunter, younger brother of the headman, Arub the Big One."

"Ah!" said the old man again, nodding. "The clan of Arub. I remember your people in the days before my knees grew weak with age and I was left to rot in my hut while others danced and feasted." His voice rose a little shrilly as he said this, but at once he sighed as if his strength was no longer sufficient for anger or anguish, and said quietly, "But your

16

home is far, young one."

"Yes, old grandfather. My home is three days' journey from here. It is near the Hills of the Killing of the Elephant."

"*Ai!*" The thin dry voice crackled and strange secret laughter began somewhere behind the wrinkles. "And did Arub the Hunter kill the elephant?"

"Yes, my grandfather. He is a great man with the bow and his arrow reaches farther than the arrows of all others." Without knowing it, he spoke with pride, but he moved uneasily in the old man's grasp.

"Stay! Stay!" whispered the old man, his grip tightening. "Your father was a great hunter of elephant, and I see that you too are a man and a warrior who wears the marks of greatness upon his body."

The boy stared up in alarm and dismay. Not only were the man's eyes dim, but his wits must surely be touched with madness also. A warrior who wore the marks of bravery in scars upon his chest? He was only a young boy who wore nothing but a patch of dressed hide dangling on a string from his loins and a charm of roots hanging on a cord round his neck which his mother had put there to guard him from evil.

He clenched his fists to give himself courage. "Old grandfather," he said. "What you say is not so for your eyes are blind and you cannot see."

He did not know if the smile faded from the old face but the folds of skin became as still as a mask, and for a long while the man was silent, gripping the boy's arm and gazing towards him with his dull white eyes.

Then at last he said, so softly that the kneeling boy could scarcely hear him, "Blind I may be, but not so blind as other men who have eyes but still cannot see. And when I look at you with these blind eyes I can see those things which others cannot perceive. I see a man who carries his head with pride...."

The old man's voice trailed away but he continued to stare towards the boy and suddenly the boy knew what he was. He was one whom men called a soothsayer, a seer into the future, one of the old respected ones who could even tell what lay ahead for a small baby. The boy's eyes grew wider with apprehension for he could not understand what was said.

"Ah, yes," said the old man. "I see that you are a seeker after glory."

17

He loosened his hold on the boy's arm, but the boy was too bewildered to move.

"So it is." Now the soothsayer's voice seemed to come from a great distance. "All men are seekers," he whispered, "but their eyes are shut like the eyes of blind men and they know not where to seek or even what it is that they seek. They stumble and fall and follow many roads. They follow many roads and still arrive at no place. But you, young one, shall walk the road to glory. I see it. I see it."

Then all at once the boy realized that he was free. Without waiting to hear more or even to be told that he might leave the hut of one who was old and respected, he turned and, scrambling through the low doorway like a bush hare, ran as fast as he could back to his grandmother.

One

Silently and swiftly Garib fitted the pointed stick into his boy's bow. He drew back the string until the muscles stood out knotted in his thin brown arms and, raising the bow to the height of his shoulders, took careful aim.

For a moment he stood there, quite still, poised on the flat slab of ironstone rock that lay among the tall white tufts of grass and the thorn trees at the foot of the low stony hill. He took a quick little breath, then let go. With a twang that went on vibrating through Garib's body and caused the village dogs to stop in their tracks and look up eagerly, the stick shot forward. It winged its way over the scrub to the tall giraffe-thorn tree. The dove in the upper branches flew up into the air in a sudden confused flash of wings. The bird flapped twice, then fell to the ground and was lost from view in the grass.

Garib did not dare to believe that he had actually hit the bird. For many moons he had been coming on his own to this deserted spot beyond the village to practise with his bow, but with no success.

He leapt off the rock and, regardless of the thorns that scratched at his legs, ran towards the tree. He stopped. The bird was lying on a patch of sand between the tufts. He could see at once that it was dead.

With a pounding heart he lifted the soft warm body in his hands.

"Down!" he shouted at the dog that was trying to thrust its nose between his fingers.

The bird's eyes were closed and its little head hung limply to the side and the bright rays of the morning sun seemed to ripple across its breast in a shining wave of pink and blue.

Feeling gently among the grey feathers, Garib found the place where his arrow stick had pierced the skin. He paused, unable to understand the quick pang of regret that passed through him or the strange feeling of hurt as if somehow he himself had received a wound.

Then, crouching on the ground, he remembered the words the old soothsayer had said to him four seasons ago at the Great Place of Games the queen. "You shall walk the road to glory." Though he had fled in fear from the old man's hut, Garib had never forgotten what the Blind One had said and though he had told no one of his experience lest they laugh, he had treasured the words secretly as his younger sister treasured a shiny white stone she had once found in the sandy river bed.

Garib pushed the small pain which he had felt at the sight of the broken bird in his hands from his mind. There was only one kind of greatness that he could think of and that was the greatness which had been won by his own father, Arub the Hunter. To be a great hunter must be glory indeed! In sudden excitement Garib wished that he could run at once to his father to show him this first kill he had made with his bow. But Arub the Hunter was not in the village. Two moons ago he had gone with the other men of the clan to take the cattle to an outpost farther north where there was still pasturage and water for the beasts in this season of severe drought. Instead, he thought, he would take the bird to his mother.

Clutching the dove, Garib walked to where his pointed stick had fallen and, picking it up, put it with the other arrows he had made in the ox-hide quiver slung across his back.

Still excited, he whistled for the dogs. They all came bounding towards him except one small brown and white bitch. She was sniffing near some boulders on the other side of the giraffe-thorn tree, her tail erect and quivering.

"Come, dog!" shouted Garib.

The dog took no notice. She was running excitedly here and there with her nose close to the dusty earth. Sniffing and snorting, with the hair on her back bristling, she followed the scent round the boulders. She stopped suddenly and began to bark, a sharp yapping bark that hurt the ears.

Garib was about to walk away, leaving the dog to find her own way home when the barking ceased and the dog gave a low howl. Crouching down with her nose between her front paws, she began to whimper softly.

The boy hesitated, then walked over to the dog. What had she found? A lost sheep? Something else? Something to fear? In apprehension Garib forgot that he was a great hunter at the beginning of his glory and became in a moment once more a young and unsure boy. Warily he looked round the rock. Lying in the dust on the other side was a man.

Garib caught his breath. The man was lying with his face downwards, naked except for his loin skins, and he was alive for every now and then his shoulders moved jerkily as he breathed. In alarm Garib looked round but there was no sign of any other men. He stared again at the still figure. There was a knife grasped in the man's hand and a patch of red blood stained the sand beside him.

"*Eisey!*" Garib whispered.

As if the man heard him, he gave a low groan.

Cautiously and fearfully Garib moved closer.

"Help me!" gasped the wounded man, moving his head so that Garib could see his face. Garib stared down in shock and disbelief. The man on the ground was his father.

"*Tatab!* Father!" he cried, dropping his bow and the dove and kneeling down. "How came you to be here?"

Arub the Hunter looked up painfully. "Garib?"

"Yes, Father!"

The man made an effort to rise, then with a groan that twisted his face, lay still once more.

"Father! My father!"

Arub the Hunter opened his eyes again and, as if it were a great effort, whispered, "Bend closer, my son. I must speak."

Garib bent right down so that his face was close to his father's. He could smell the sweat and the blood of his body and the odour was so frightening that he wished suddenly to flee.

"My child. ... Listen well for you must take my words to my brother, Arub the Big One, in the village."

21

"First let me run to fetch help, *Tatab*, for I see you are wounded."

"No!" The word came out loudly for Garib had already started to rise.

Dread clutched at Garib's throat and he had to force himself to bend close again. "Yes, my father."

Arub the Hunter said, "I have been running for two days and now I can run no further." He gasped the words out one by one. "Garib!"

"I am here, father."

"Tell Arub the Big One that the Cattle People are coming. They attacked the outpost as day was dawning.... They killed everyone.... Took away all the cattle. They left me for dead ... wounded and hidden beneath the sheepskin blankets."

The Cattle People! The tall Black Men who owned great herds of cattle! Garib had heard of these people from the travellers who came to trade iron goods for sheep and oxen in the village. He knew they were an enemy for they were not of the nation of the Men of Men, but he had never thought of them as a danger.

"But, *Tatab*," he whispered as Arub paused to gather strength. "The Cattle People live in the valleys to the far north. They live beyond the great mountains."

Arub gazed unseeingly at Garib as if he had not heard, then he said, "The drought ... the drought which forced us to take our cattle north in search of grass and water ... forced the Cattle People to come south. They are coming ... killing ... killing."

For a few moments Arub the Hunter was unable to speak, then he whispered, "Closer! Come closer for my strength is failing and I am dying."

Garib leant ever nearer until he could feel his father's quick gasps of breath on his face.

"My son," said Arub the Hunter. "Tell Arub the Big One ... there is no time to lose. He must flee with the people before it is too late ... before the Hills of the Killing of the Elephant become the Hills of the Killing of Men."

"Yes, my father, I shall go now."

"Wait!" Blood trickled from the man's mouth. "Listen! The man among the Cattle People who did this thing is named Kahitjene. Do you hear, Garib? Kahitjene!"

"Yes, my father." Garib could feel tears of despair gathering in his eyes.

Arub the Hunter drew a shuddering breath and went on. "There were servants of the nation of the Mountain People among the Cattle People ... They spoke the language of the Men of Men ... I heard them say it was Kahitjene who had sent his men to take our grazing lands ..." With a tremendous effort the dying man pushed himself up into a half-sitting position as if anger gave him strength. "Do you hear, one who is my son?" he gasped. "Soon I shall be dead and it is the law of our people that blood must pay for blood ... When you are a man you must seek for this Kahitjene so that you may kill him. This you must do and this you shall do though it takes you all the days of your life!"

Garib's father stopped abruptly, then, panting, he held out his knife. "Take this to my brother—" But he could not finish the sentence. A sudden look of fury flashed in his eye. The blade fell from his hand and landed with a soft thud in the dust, and the next moment, with a great sigh, he fell back and lay still.

Trembling, Garib looked at him. Arub the Hunter's eyes were open but they were staring up unseeingly at the sky. Garib made no sound. He remained kneeling beside the dead man for a while, then cautiously he reached out and picked up the knife. And suddenly panic burst in him. Forgotten was the bow he had left beside the boulder on the hill, and forgotten too was the grey dove, his first kill. With the dogs leaping and barking at his heels, he raced wildly across the flat lands, across the dry river bed, to the high ground beyond where the village lay.

Garib found Arub the Big One squatting outside his hut smoking with Tomarib his Counsellor and some of the older men who had remained behind with the women and children in the village when the young men had taken the cattle to better pasturage.

23

"*Khub!* My chief!" he cried, gasping for breath. "The Cattle People are coming! The Cattle People are coming!" He hardly knew what he was saying in his haste and shock.

Arub the Big One, always quick to anger, paused as he was about to take a puff at the smoking horn. "What is this you say?"

"My chief! My father lies dead of his wounds upon the hillside and all our men in the north are killed by the Cattle People and all the cattle are stolen!"

"*Ai!*" The Big One's eyes narrowed to slits in his sharp face and his cruel mouth opened in a snarl of indignation at Garib's jumbled words. "You lie!" he screamed. "How can the herdsmen be dead? Such things do not happen to the Men of Men!"

"No, no, my Lord! It is true. I swear it. Here is my father's knife." Garib held out the blade.

Arub the Big One took the knife and his anger turned to blank astonishment, and all the men about him were speechless as they gazed at the carved handle which carried on it the marks of Arub the Hunter.

Then everyone was shouting at once. "What has happened? Who is dead?" The women, hearing the noise came hurrying out of the huts and even the children left their games and came crowding round.

"Silence!" Tomarib held up his hand. He was an old man and his face had that folded and puckered look which came to people when their teeth were worn to stumps, and the tufts of beard upon his chin were white and wispy with age, but his mouth was straight and stern and his eyes, as he turned to Garib, were calm, the eyes of a man who knew how men should act. Not for nothing had Tomarib been chosen to advise the chief.

"My child," said Tomarib. "Tell us what you know."

Garib's panic grew less under the old man's steady gaze.

"Old father," he said, forcing himself to speak out bravely and clearly as he knew Tomarib expected him to do. "While I was practising with my bow on the hill beyond the river I found my father dying among the boulders. He was on his way to the village to warn the people but his strength failed."

24

As Garib went on to repeat all that his father had told him many of the women whose men had gone north with the cattle, began weeping loudly in distress. Still dazed, Garib looked towards them and saw his mother with his little sister clinging to her leather skirt. She was a strong woman who had never been one to show her feelings, and even now Garib saw that her eyes were dry and staring, her face hard with a grief that was too deep for tears.

Over and over Garib had to tell the story as the men questioned him, each asking him to repeat what Arub the Hunter had said as if hoping for some new words which might alter the meaning of his message.

Then Arub the Big One leapt forward. "We will walk against these Cattle People!" he cried. "We shall kill these dogs who have dared to do this thing to our people!"

"*Ai! Ai! Ai!*" Angry shouts arose from all sides. "We shall kill these Black Men who have come down from the far north into our grazing lands and we shall get back our cattle!"

There was so much noise and commotion that it was some time before Tomarib could make himself heard again.

"Such talk is nothing but foolishness," he shouted, and when at last the people were quiet he put his hand on the Big One's arm and said, "What nonsense is this to speak of fighting the Cattle People? How can we go to war when most of our young men have been killed? There are only a few hunters who stayed behind to keep the village supplied with fresh game." He turned to the men and said sternly, "Have you forgotten your age, old ones? We must do as Arub the Hunter has told us. We must flee."

At this reproach many of the men looked shame-faced like small boys caught out in some mischief, and Garib heard one say, "*Ai!* Tomarib is right. The Black Men are too strong for us for it is said that they eat much meat." But Arub the Big One's face was convulsed with rage. It was well known that he hated the old Counsellor whom the people had chosen to advise him and who so often showed him to be nothing but a hot-blooded fool.

He jerked to free himself from Tomarib's restraining hand. "You are nothing but old women dressed in the clothes of

25

men!" he shouted at the people. "And you, Tomarib," his voice was sharp with anger and scorn, "you say we must flee. But to which place shall we flee, wise old man? The way to the east is barred by the clan of Moreb. What man would be so stupid as to set his foot on their hunting lands?"

"Yes," said Tomarib calmly. "It is true that we cannot flee east to reach the Great Place of Games the queen for your quarrelling has made enemies of the clan of Moreb. The west also is blocked by the great desert. We shall have to flee to the south."

"The south!" The Big One's voice rose to a scream. "Do you forget the drought which caused us even here to send our cattle to the north? To the south lies the Land of Sand and Stone. There is no water there until the rains come. To travel south is to die of thirst on the plains!"

Tomarib nodded slowly. "It is as you say," he said. "If we flee to the south some of our people may die of thirst, but some shall surely reach the southern fountains. If we stay or try to fight the Cattle People it shall be as The Hunter has said. The hills of the Killing of the Elephant shall become the Hills of the Killing of Men and we shall all perish."

Arub opened his mouth to retort, then as if he could find no further argument to use against Tomarib, he closed it again. He shrugged and his mouth twisted into a kind of smile. "As always you are right," he said bitterly. "I am a chief without warriors. A man cannot fight with honour when he has only old women to carry the bows. Once again you have shown me my foolishness, Tomarib, and we shall go south for there is nowhere else we may go." He started to walk away, then turned back. "But hear me!" he cried. "I shall not forget the hurt which these Cattle People have done to me. One day I shall return and then I will show them what happens to those who steal cattle from Arub the Big One!"

And as he stood beside the men Garib clenched his fists. In a jumble of thoughts he remembered his father's words about Kahitjene and saw again Arub the Hunter's dead face and his mother's grief-stricken eyes. I too shall return, he vowed, but he was still too confused and numbed with shock to know clearly even what he thought.

Two

On the morning of the second day after Garib had brought
the news of the coming of the Cattle People, the clan of Arub
was up at the first light, making the final preparations for the
long journey. The men, women and children worked together
to take down the huts, roll the rush mats of the roofs, make
the thin supple boughs of the framework into bundles and
tie their packed up houses on to the waiting pack-oxen. Then
the waterbags were filled at the muddy waterhole in the
river bed and all that was left of the cooked bulbs and other
veld food, and the long strings of meat that had been dried
in the sun were put into net baskets and secured with leather
thongs to the bundles. Long forked sticks were bound to the
sides of the oxen to carry the earthen cooking pots and milk
calabashes, and, last of all, the smaller children were lifted up
and placed one behind the other on top of the sheepskin
blankets on the backs of the laden beasts. On other pack-oxen
the rest of the pots and possessions were fastened, and those
who were too old or too weak to go on foot were helped on to
the sheepskin saddles of the ride-oxen, and when everything
was in readiness the clan set off across the plain towards the
blue-grey mountains in the south, led by one who knew the
way. The long terrible journey which Garib was to remember
all his life had begun.

Following Arub the Big One, Tomarib and the guide came
the rest of the people, some on oxen, some on foot, the women
with their skin cloaks tied up for walking and the men wearing their fur caps, their bows slung over their shoulders, their

27

arrows and knobbed clubs in the quivers on their backs, and their spears in their hands. And behind the people was the long line of pack-oxen and the few other cattle and milch cows which had not been driven to the northern outpost, herded by the Mountain People servants, and then came Garib and the other boys driving the sheep and goats before them.

This was not the first time the people of Arub had been forced to move their village. Even in the eleven seasons of Garib's life they had lifted up their huts three times to move on to better pasturage. They were used to wandering across the plains of great Namaland. But never before had they trekked southward, away from the places they knew, and sadness hung like a cloud over the procession as it went slowly over the dry plain.

The first day they passed through country which was familiar to Garib. The low grey scrub interspersed between the small thorn bushes provided sufficient grazing for the sheep and goats, and here and there taller giraffe-thorn trees with rough twisted trunks and thick grey-green foliage, held high, gave welcome patches of shade when the sun reached its height. And as they went they passed two giraffes, their long orange necks showing above the trees, and a great kudu tossed its mighty horns at the sight of the men, and later they came upon a group of beautiful springbok which bounded away as they approached, leaping over the bushes as light and airy as if they were being blown by the wind. But though the men's fingers itched to reach for their bows, they knew they could not stop to hunt. They had food enough in their bags and must hurry on to reach the next waterhole.

Even by the afternoon the people began to realize the severity of the drought. The undergrowth became thinner. There were wide expanses of pale gold sand with sparsely scattered rust brown scrub and thorn bushes, which in the dryness of the season had become tangles of long white thorns. The few giraffe-thorn trees to be seen were stunted, and the weary flocks, moving slowly across the veld, looked like ghostly spirits coming out of the fine clouds of dust raised by their little hooves.

And when at last they reached the waterhole on the second day they found it was half empty. When they had refilled their bags there was only enough muddy liquid left in the hole to water a quarter of their oxen and none of the sheep or goats at all.

"The next water is the Pool of the Buffalo, my *khub*," said the guide, staring down into the pit, his thick lips pursed and his leathery brown face screwed up in thought. "It is two days distant."

"Then we must move on," snarled Arub the Big One. "The beasts are thirsty."

Pausing only to camp during the hours of darkness, the long procession hurried on as quickly as the slow flocks would allow. They reached the southern mountains and passed through a kloof where stone-strewn koppies rose sharply on either side, burnt by the scorching sun to a dark red-brown. Nothing grew between the stones. The slopes were completely bare except for some grey broken branches in the crevices, as if the shrubs had sought refuge there from the sun and died in a last twisted torture of thirst.

Gazing at this desolation, the people of Arub began to feel real fear. Some of them had travelled south before in other years but now they saw that indeed the drought lay like a dead hand upon the land.

When they came through the kloof, they stopped and stared at the great plain that lay before them. It stretched as far as the eye could see, from the low dunes on the fringe of the Great Desert in the west to the horizon in the east, flat and endless, the stunted grey-brown scrub peppered over the yellow sand like the crinkled tufts of hair on an old man's head, and here and there wide patches of small white stones that reflected the sun's rays lay shimmering in a dazzling haze. No living thing moved. It was the silent Land of Sand and Stone.

"No people can cross such a land," said the Big One, scowling at Tomarib as if to blame him, but even his anger was subdued as if man could not help but know his own smallness when he stood upon so vast a plain.

Tomarib looked solemn, but his gaze did not waver. "We

must go on, my chief," he said, "and we must go speedily for the waterbags are empty."

Most of the cattle had now been for four days without water and their distress was already very great. They were standing with drooping heads, their flanks hollow and every now and then they gave low moans as if their suffering was too much to bear and as the people began to move on some of the oxen stumbled with weakness.

The further south they went the drier and more silent the land became. Under the grey surface of the soil orange patches showed, and here and there curious hills rose up on the vast flatness which were nothing but huge piles of orange boulders. There was no grass, only leafless scrub, the branches of which were like long thin fingers reaching for the sky and an occasional thorn tree, grey-white in its haze of thorns as if it had been burnt and was covered with fine white ash. In the distance soft hills of red sand were beginning to form as if already the dreaded dunes of the desert were starting to claim this land as their own. And there was no sound except that made by the labouring people as they struggled onwards. There was no game, no buck or zebra to stir the dust of the plain, no birds circling in the immense white sky.

On and on they went under a burning sun and still there was no sign of the promised water.

"You have led us astray!" gasped Arub between parched lips, grabbing the guide by the neck as if he would kill him.

"No, no, my chief," whimpered the little guide. "The people walk too slowly. Soon we come to the Pool of the Buffalo. There! There!" With a quivering finger he pointed to a range of dark mountains in the distance. "It lies in that direction."

Some of the old people who could walk no more sat down on the ground and did not rise when the rest moved on. One or two of the women turned to stare at them, grief upon their faces, but no word was said. They knew that in this cruel land it was the law that the strongest must survive, and that if those who still had strength did not go on, all would die in the barren wilderness and the clan of Arub would disappear from the earth.

30

They stumbled on. Their lips swollen and cracked from thirst, their tongues stuck to the roofs of their mouths and they were no longer able to eat the meat that was rotting in their bags. It was not until the morning of the next day that they sighted a grey-green patch on the earth far ahead. With pitiful eagerness the people struggled to hurry.

"It is strange," whispered Tomarib. Because of his age he could do no more than totter in his exhaustion. "The cattle do not stampede as thirsty cattle do when they smell water."

Some of the younger men had gone on ahead of the others. They came to a slight rise in the flat plain from where they could look down into the pool. The people behind could not understand why they had stopped, then from one man to the next the word was passed back. "There is no water in the Pool of the Buffalo! There is no water!"

In horror and disbelief the rest of the clan joined the men on the ridge. What had once been a lake was now nothing but a wide hollowed basin in the ground, the clay of its cracked surface tinged green and shining in the sun.

For a moment no one moved, then Tomarib, taking a digging stick from the sling bag of one of the women, staggered down the slope into the centre of the hollow and began to dig. The others crowded round him. The deeper Tomarib dug, the drier the sand became.

At last Tomarib laid the digging stick aside and sank down panting on to the cracked clay.

The Big One stared down into the dry hole, then he turned to Tomarib and even though his tongue was swollen so that he spoke thickly, he still managed to twist his mouth into a bitter smile. "You are the one chosen to advise, Old One. Advise us now!"

The people looked at Tomarib, seeking guidance in their distress, but the old man remained sitting with his head bent and they saw that his wisdom had been drained from him as the waters had been drained from the lake. He was too old and his suffering was too great.

Slowly he lifted his head and mumbled, "If we go on and do not find water we shall all die. And if we go back we shall also die for the way is too far for us in our weakness."

The people stared at the old counsellor in silence and despair sank down upon them too. Some of them sat down beside Tomarib.

In only one face life remained. It was as if anger alone now kept Arub the Big One on his feet.

"I will not allow my people to die while there is yet strength in them to walk on," he said. And as he spoke he brought his knobbed club down on Tomarib's shoulders. "Stand, man!" he screamed, his voice cracking and squeaking through his parched lips. "Stand and walk or I shall kill you like a dog!"

Like a madman the Big One went from one man to the next with his club rising and falling upon the heads and shoulders of his people until once more they were standing in line.

Beating the cattle to make them move on also, the people set off again across the plain. As far as the eye could see there was neither bush nor tree. The country seemed covered with stones, with here and there a patch of grey sand and gravel, and single blades of grass bending under the burning sun. Even the mountains in the distance looked black and forbidding as if they too were charred by death.

By noon the heat became unbearable. The cattle halted every few steps and, with drooping heads and protruding tongues, tried in vain to bellow. One by one the oxen and the sheep and goats dropped down and not even the rod could rouse them. The dogs too no longer knew their names or came to the call of their masters. Their eyes seemed shrunk to mere specks under their shaggy brows and at times blood flowed from their nostrils as they glided on in silence.

Then the people too began to fall down. Their skins dry, their eyes bloodshot and their mouths covered with a crust, they lay helpless and dying, some crying in the madness and agony of their thirst.

"Leave them!" whispered the Big One, his voice hardly more than a croak as Garib stopped beside his dying grandmother in bewilderment.

Garib's throat was closed with dryness so that he could

32

scarcely breathe. He looked towards his mother, but she was staring ahead with dull eyes, still clutching the hand of his young sister as if her whole strength were flowing from her to the child and she had no more to give to anyone else.

"Walk on, I say!" hissed Arub, gripping Garib's arm and dragging him away.

Garib staggered forward and in his confusion of thirst he did not even look back. In front of him was Fast Foot, one of the hunters who had stayed behind at the village to provide the people with game. He was a young man and had received his name because he could run more swiftly than any other man. Now he could hardly even walk. Like one in a daze Garib watched Fast Foot's thin knotted legs moving with painful, listless steps, and after a while a great drowsiness overtook him so that he could scarcely force one foot before the other and he no longer knew where he was going or even why.

Then at last Garib felt a coolness on his body. They had reached the black mountain and had halted in the shadow of a great rock that jutted out from its side. The people sank down in the sand and Garib, vaguely aware that his mother and sister were sitting in the shade, sank down too.

He lay down in the sand and closed his eyes for somewhere inside him was a pain. And then his vagueness became like a dream and he thought he heard the sound of running water, and felt the coolness of the water running over his body.

And in this strange dream scenes from his own life seemed to flow past him. He saw the old soothsayer who had spoken to him of glory, and then suddenly he saw the dove which he had killed with his boy's arrow. It was the first time he had thought of it since finding his father. Sadness washed over him like a wave. He had hoped that this might be the beginning of his glory, but now he knew that it was, instead, the end. It was the end of everything.

"Kahitjene," he murmured with his lips in the sand. He stirred restlessly. "Kahitjene. Kahitjene."

Then the pain seemed to swell up and consume even his thoughts. He slept and woke, slept and woke, and when he woke again the pain had gone. There was only a great greyness

33

and a great sadness everywhere and he felt that he was going to die.

He turned on to his back and opened his eyes. He gazed up into the sky but he did not try to move. And as he stared up faint black specks began to appear in the greyness. They became larger and larger and increased in size until they became winged creatures resembling flies at that great height. Stupidly Garib went on gazing at them.

The black specks came lower still and formed themselves into a wide ring far above, and suddenly Garib knew what they were. They were vultures, circling round their prey and waiting to know that it was dead before they dared to swoop down to their awful feast.

Garib lifted his arm to shield himself against the thought of the vicious tearing beaks and as he moved life seemed to stir in him once more and sense flowed again into his brain. He took his hand away and looked up in amazement at the circle of vultures which was growing as more and more birds came rushing to join it. Then, pushing his hands against the ground to give him strength to rise, he sat up.

"My chief!" he whispered. "My chief! Look!" With a trembling hand he pointed upwards. "Vultures!" He had no need to say more for all men of the desert lands knew that where there was vultures, there must be game, and where there was game, there must also be water.

They found the water on the other side of the black mountain. There the earth was no longer burnt orange. It was grey and covered with scattered trees and bush, and pale yellow grass grew in close tufts upon it, and winding across the plain was a dark line of bush marking the twisting path of a river.

Stumbling and staggering and weeping, the people ran to the large pool in the dry bed as if they had been crazed. Falling and crawling, they threw themselves into the water and lay in it, drinking and drinking until it ran out of their mouths again. But still they could not seem to quench their thirst and even when they were writhing with agony from the effects of too much water too quickly, they kept crawling back for more.

34

But even when at last Garib's thirst was eased and he lay helpless and weak upon the bank one word kept repeating itself over and over in his head. Kahitjene. Kahitjene. It was Kahitjene who had done this to his people.

Three

Too weary to go further in search of a new home, the few who were left of the clan of Arub stayed beside the waterhole, for the water was clean and plentiful, and there was veld food to be found under the hard crust of earth, and the game, though not abundant on the dry plain, was sufficient.

And so they continued to live behind the black mountain, but though the place where they camped soon began to have something of the appearance of a village, it was not like their old home. The people did not build proper huts or sew together reeds for neat mats for the roofs. They only threw up shelters of rough branches on the high ground beyond the waterhole as men might do when out hunting and caught by the night. And they did not dance when the moon was full or pray to Tsui-Goab or do any of those things which had been an accepted part of their old life. It was as if the spirit had gone out of them and they thought of nothing but of how to find enough food to fill their stomachs.

Then one day as the men were sitting beside the fire, cutting up the carcase of a zebra which Fast Foot had chased and killed with his hunting knife, Arub the Big One stood up suddenly and, narrowing his eyes, stared into the distance.

"What is that?" he asked, pointing to a faint cloud of dust across the plain.

At once Fast Foot put down his iron blade and reached for his bow, his large face earnest and anxious, but the other men, eager for the feast, hardly paused in their work. The zebra had already been skinned and the men were hacking great hunks from the bones and, with swift spiralling movements of their knives, cutting long strips of red meat. Many of these strips already hung in festoons from the branches of the nearby trees and bushes to dry in the sun so that they might be preserved for later use, other great coils were fizzling on the fire beside the big clay pots where the most delicate morsels were bubbling and steaming.

"It does not look like buffalo," said Fast Foot slowly, wrinkling his forehead like a puzzled dog.

Now some of the other men, their curiosity aroused, joined Fast Foot and the Big One. With their mouths stuffed with half-cooked meat they watched the dust cloud coming closer, and the women, leaving their tasks, came to stand with them, their eyes sharp with apprehension, and Garib put down the stone with which he was pounding bones to extract the marrow and came to the front of his mother's hut where he too could see.

Moving at speed across the plain the cloud was coming straight towards the waterhole. At first nothing could be seen but dust, then as it came still nearer Garib could make out moving legs and dark shapes in the haze.

"It is horses!" shouted Arub the Big One. "It is men on horses."

"Horses!" Hastily some of the men fitted arrows into their bows.

Garib stared at the confusion of hooves and dust in alarm not a little tinged with eagerness. He had heard of horses and also of these men who rode them, but he had never before seen them. Only Arub the Big One and Tomarib who had journeyed to the Great Place of Games the queen to take the yearly tributes had met some of these people and they had told the clan of Arub about these strangers.

It was said that they were Men of Men who had gone south across the Great River many generations ago, and now, driven back by strange powerful people with white skins who lived there, they were returning in bands to the plains of Namaland. Tomarib had said that they wore peculiar clothing and owned unknown weapons called guns which they had obtained from the White Men, and the people at the Great Place had called them "wearers of hats" and had spoken of them with hidden

37

scorn for it was whispered that they were nothing but robbers and they had come to beg for hunting lands from Games. As the men of Arub watched the strangers approaching their eyes were filled with suspicion.

At last with a thundering of hooves on the hard earth and a surge of dust and a whinnying and snorting of beasts, the horsemen came to a halt not more than ten paces from the waiting men. As the dust settled Garib saw that there were ten horsemen. The clothing they wore was indeed strange and on their heads were unfamiliar hats with wide brims, and under their arms were long metal weapons glancing in the sunlight.

A man in their midst raised a hand in salute and called out, "Greetings! I did not know there were people living here. I thought the land was empty, but I saw the smoke from your fires and have brought some of my men here in search of water."

By the way the man spoke Garib realized that he must be the chief among these people. He stared up at him, aware of a slight disappointment for the man was small and slender and, in spite of his strange clothing and the fearsome beast he rode, he seemed no different from any other man. He had the same high cheek bones, the same narrow-lidded eyes and prominent lips, the same yellow-brown skin. Only his nose seemed longer and thinner than most, but there was nothing else to show that he was anything but an ordinary man of the Men of Men. Even Arub the Big One looked much fiercer and, glancing quickly at his own chief, Garib saw that Arub too was seeing the man's smallness and that already the first signs of scorn were beginning to chase out the fear which had been in his face.

"Greetings!" said the Big One. "I am Arub the Big One, chief of the clan of Arub. We were driven from our home in the north by the Cattle People and have been living here for nearly two summers."

"*Ai!*" The little chief showed great interest in the Big One's words and seemed eager to hear more, but, as if remembering that proper greetings had not yet been exchanged, he leapt from his horse and approached Arub.

"I am Haramub," he said, speaking in the Nama tongue. "I am the chief of the *Aich-ai*, the Warlike People. I am also called Jonker Afrikaner for this was the name given to me by the white people south of the Great River." As he spoke, the words sounded like a boast and he looked round quickly as if to discover if this name had any meaning to the men of Arub.

"You are welcome to my house, Haramub of the Warlike People," said the Big One. Now his scorn was more pronounced, as if he saw that this was a little man who longed for greatness, but his glance kept moving to the large gun under Haramub's arm and it was clear that it was only his fear of this unknown weapon that kept his words polite.

Haramub looked at him shrewdly, then suddenly his eyes hardened as if he did not like scorn. Deliberately he turned away from the Big One and gazed at the village. "This is your home?" he asked and there was no need for even a hint of a sneer to convey his meaning.

Ai! This stranger might be small, but he was clever—and bold. Garib saw the Big One's thin face flush with anger, and Garib too felt his cheeks burning with shame as he followed Haramub's gaze. He seemed to see the village for the first time. Why, it was more like the house of one of the wild Bushmen than a home of the Men of Men.

Arub the Big One opened his mouth as if to speak in fury as was his habit at any insult, even one which was not directly expressed, then his glance went quickly again towards the man's gun and he bit back the hot retort. Instead he kicked viciously at a dog which had sidled up to him, then screamed at the women to bring honey beer for his guests in a voice that set the people running in all directions.

Haramub watched, his unblinking eyes seeming to miss nothing, then slowly he smiled and signalled to his men to dismount and tether the horses to the nearby trees.

"Tell your people also to bring water for my horses," he told Arub, "and in a short while the rest of my tribe will be here with my cattle. They too shall need refreshment for I am on my way to a place south of the clan of Hobesen, for this is where the queen Games has given me land."

In all his life Garib had never heard Arub the Big One

spoken to like this, as if he were a servant. And by one who was homeless and a stranger in the land! Indeed he saw that he had been wrong to think this little chief an ordinary man. With a quick thrill of excitement and fear Garib moved closer.

Sullenly Arub the Big One led the strangers back to the tall giraffe-thorn tree in the centre of the village where the men had been cutting up the zebra, and soon all were drinking beer and eating meat and veld food which the women brought to them in dishes. And when Haramub's cattle arrived, the rest of his men joined those at the fire and as the beer pots were passed round yet again the contest of will between Haramub and Arub the Big One seemed forgotten in the general talk and laughter.

"Bring the pipe, son of my brother!" shouted the Big One, and Garib, bounding up with eagerness, raced off to the chief's hut and returned with the long smoking horn. With quick fingers he filled the small dish in the side of the pipe with hemp leaves and, taking a burning root from the fire, placed his mouth to the open end of the horn. He drew a deep breath so that the leaves crackled as the flame caught and a cloud of dense smoke came up into Garib's mouth. He had lit the pipe many times before for the men and though his head reeled with the sweet heady fumes and his eyes filled with blinding tears, he managed not to choke. He did not wish this strange, exciting little chief to find *him* stupid also.

When the pipe was drawing well Garib handed it to Arub the Big One, then crouched just behind the ring of men where he could listen to the talk without being chased away.

"You say, Big One, that you were driven from your home in the north by the Cattle People," said Haramub after the pipe had been passed round. "I have heard of these Angry People." He leant forward as if he felt that the time had come to pursue this subject which had so obviously interested him. "I have heard that their land beyond the mountains is a place of good pasturage and plentiful water where men seldom know the agony of thirst. I have heard too that their herds of cattle are so great that they cover the hills like grass. But it is said that they are nothing but dogs, these Black Men who defeated

40

you and chased you from your homes."

Like a fire which has been smouldering out of sight under the logs of the hearth but is suddenly fanned back into life, Arub's anger flared up again. And now Garib saw with quick apprehension that his eyes were glazed with the courage of hemp also. He snatched the pipe from Tomarib and drew on it so deeply that the smoke billowed out from between the rim of the horn and his lips and he coughed and choked to such an extent that Fast Foot had to pour water upon him to revive him.

When the Big One could speak again he stared at Haramub with eyes that were mere pinpoints of hatred. "You speak with a glib tongue, stranger!" he shouted. "But I tell you this, it is better to hear of these Cattle People than to see them! They are twice the size of a puny man like you and the travellers say they carry spears as broad as your head." He spluttered again from smoke and anger, then went on. "I see by the look on your face that you are greedy for the wealth of these dogs, but I tell you that you had better forget such madness. If Arub the Big One fled before them, how can a man such as you, with no home and so small a tribe, hope to stand against them?"

The people of Arub stared aghast at their chief. No one dared to speak and in fear they watched Haramub pick up the gun that lay beside him and get to his feet.

"Wait, stranger!" cried Tomarib, stepping forward. Ever since the long walk the old man had been quiet and brooding as if the memory of his failure to advise the people bravely at the time of their greatest need haunted him. He had been like a broken man. But now he roused himself and looked almost like the old counsellor Garib remembered. "Sire," he said. "Do not heed the words of our chief. He is drunk with hemp or he could not speak such foolishness."

Haramub's arms did not pause as they lifted the heavy weapon, but he glanced towards Tomarib. "Do not fear, good father," he said grimly. "I mean no harm to your people."

As the men of Arub watched with growing apprehension, he brought the gun level with his shoulder, but he did not point it at the man who had insulted him. He was aiming it at

41

a bright yellow and orange parrot that was sitting on the topmost branch of a thorn tree near the pool some distance in front of the huts. Haramub's finger moved. There was a flash of flame and a puff of smoke and a sound like the deafening crash of thunder.

The men of Arub hid their heads in consternation and the women ran screaming into their huts. When the smoke had cleared Garib saw that the parrot was gone.

Haramub put down the gun and turned to Garib. "Fetch the bird," he said.

Garib gaped at him for a moment, then, scrambling up and almost falling over his own feet in his alarm, ran in haste to the spot where the parrot had fallen. He picked it up and, running back, laid it breathlessly at Haramub's feet.

Arub the Big One's eyes were rolling. *"Eisey!"* he whispered. "I have heard of these weapons, but I did not know their power."

Haramub looked down calmly. "Yes, Arub. It is better to have heard of guns than to have seen them," he said, mimicking the chief's tone. "A gun may kill a bird at a distance and it may also kill a man. When I was in the south I learnt from the White Men and I know that a man with a true gun and a fast horse may kill many people and remain unharmed. He may also drive away many cattle."

The sound of the explosion seemed to have cleared even the effects of the hemp smoke from the Big One's brain and he had nothing to say.

"Yes, Arub," said Haramub again, his eyes bright and iron-hard. "My people are homeless and few for the White Men have chased us from our lands, but we have brought their guns and horses with us and we shall not live long as a tributary people on these arid southern plains. One day the great lands to the north shall be my land and the vast herds of the Cattle People shall be the herds of the one they call Jonker Afrikaner!"

The people of Arub stared at Haramub and even some of his own men gaped at this enormous boast, but no one dared to laugh. Some of them might think him touched with madness to dream even of such greatness, but in Haramub's eyes

42

there was such purpose and determination that they dared not even smile.

Then suddenly Haramub picked up his hat. "But do not be afraid, Big One," he said. "If you do not stand in my way, I shall do you no harm. Instead, to thank you for your hospitality, I shall give you six fat cows in milk and two fine bulls from my own herds so that your people may grow strong and rich again for one day I shall need brave men to help me." And calling to his herdsmen to fetch the cattle for Arub, he began to walk away from the huts to the bushes where the horses were tethered. With one twist of his slim supple body he was upon his horse's back and raising his arm in farewell.

Garib watched him in dazed admiration. He thought he had never seen a man like this before. Surely this was how a man of courage should be. Haramub's great dream of glory seemed to shimmer like some marvellous mirage upon the desert sands in front of Garib's eyes. And in a moment he would be gone and then there would be nothing again but the lowly shameful village and the despair!

Several of the children were running out to watch the men mount their horses and suddenly Garib was running too, his heart pounding wildly with excitement. He hardly knew what he meant to do. He could only think of Haramub's words, "One day I shall need brave men to help me."

"My chief! My chief!" He reached the big brown stallion and threw himself in its path. "Let me come with you. Let me come with you. I shall help you to fight against the Cattle People!"

Haramub pulled sharply on the reins. The horse whinnied and stamped in the dust. The little man looked down in surprise.

"You want to come with me to kill the Cattle People?"

"Yes, my chief. It was Kahitjene of the Cattle People who killed my father, Arub the Hunter!"

Haramub gazed down from his great height. "But you are only a child!" he exclaimed. Then suddenly he threw back his head and laughed.

The sound was like a lash across Garib's face. Blinding tears stung his eyes. Not even noticing the snorting beast so close to him, he hung his head.

Then the laughter ceased.

"Who are you, boy?"

Garib forced himself to look up. "I am Garib, son of Arub the Hunter," he said.

Haramub smiled and his teeth flashed white in his small brown face, but his expression was not unkind. "So, Garib, son of Arub the Hunter," he said. "Do not be sad for I shall remember you for I see that you are a boy of spirit. Come to me again when you are a man for I may have need of you!"

Then quickly he turned his horse and was galloping away across the plain with his horsemen. Feeling as dizzy and light-headed as if he had suddenly awoken from a wild dream, Garib stood there gazing after the fast-disappearing cloud of dust, and remembering the stranger's words to him he was filled with wonder.

Four

Though Arub the Big One remained sullen and resentful for some days so that he beat his servants and kicked at his dogs and shouted at his people, it seemed that the visit of Haramub had made him think. The very next day he told the men to go out and cut down supple branches and ordered the women to collect reeds from the waterhole so that they could build proper huts and the village of Arub might no longer be like the home of a wild man from the bush.

The people too seemed to come alive again. They made pots and prepared skins for clothing and sought for clay pits so that they could refill their boxes of red ochre with which fine men greased their skins.

And as if drawn to the village by its growing prosperity, refugees, remnants of tribes driven south also by the advance of the Cattle People, began to arrive to seek for shelter and swell the numbers of the clan of Arub. Among them was a doctor of the spirits, a *gei-nun*, and then the people were once more able to dance to the moon and to sing praises to Tsui-Goab, the Great Creator, and could live like a proper people with a god.

They were also able to receive news for, though the Great Place of the queen was too far for them to journey there at the time of the making of rain, travellers and traders called at the village. They heard from them of how the Cattle People were swarming into the Place of the Elephants and were driving the Men of Men back even from the land south of the Kuiseb River. Some of the clans had tried to stand against the tall Black Men and had been destroyed for their courage. More and more of the land upon which the foot of the Nama

45

hunter and herdsman had trod and which by ancient law they had a right to claim as their own, was being taken from them, but even in this danger the quarrels between the different chiefs of the Nama nation kept them from banding together to repulse their powerful foe.

Then one day news of the One with Two Names reached them. A trader in spears and iron arrow points told them that Games the queen in her despair had asked for the help of Haramub who was also called Jonker Afrikaner. Garib came close and stood listening, the beat of his heart quickening at the mention of this man who had made such an impact upon him.

"The people used to pretend to have scorn for the men from the south," the trader was saying, "but anyone who scorns Haramub is a fool. I tell you, his father lived along the Great River for many seasons and he was a very fierce man until he died. The clans all around would leave their homes and take to the bush if they heard he was near for they said they would rather face the beasts of prey in the hills than gaze upon this lion and hear his roar. And this man, Haramub, who lived with the White Men, is his father's son. Men say he has the eyes of a leopard and that the Cattle People will soon tremble before the fire of his guns."

The eyes of a leopard, thought Garib, and remembering the little chief's hard, unblinking stare he thought the description was true. He longed to hear more but indeed it seemed that men knew little of Haramub. It was said that Haramub himself would never speak of his past, like a man who had secrets to hide, and the only other news Garib could learn was that the strange little chief had demanded of Games the right to choose his own land in which to live as payment for his help and that he had now gone north with his men and horses to seek the enemy.

But though little was known of Haramub, much was spoken. Even Arub the Big One suddenly forgot his hatred and jealousy of the stranger from the south and began to boast loudly to all who would listen of how Haramub had given him cattle and was his friend. No one now called the Warlike People robbers. In one season, it seemed, the little chief had

46

become something of a hero, the one to whom everyone looked to save their land.

Then as time passed and nothing was heard of Haramub except that he had driven back a small clan of Black Men from the central plains and had built his house there, the people began to forget their sudden champion again, and Garib, who had reached the age of fourteen summers, was told that he must learn to be a hunter. Arub the Big One gave him a man's bow and appointed Fast Foot to teach him. And then even Garib began to forget the little man who had inspired him with such thoughts of glory. All his life he had lived for the day when he would become a real hunter. Had his own father not been Arub the Hunter?

But a boy could not learn to be a hunter quickly, and Fast Foot, though as fast as a buck at running, was slow at all else. He was a man of great caution who would take the whole of a morning to sharpen his hunting knife on a piece of stone, or the whole of a day to mix the juices for the poison for his arrows, and after a while Garib, though grateful for Fast Foot's endless patience and good nature, wondered if the time of watching and waiting would ever be over.

First he had to learn to know the marks left by the beasts upon the sand among the stones and by the bushes, marks which a careless eye would not notice. He had to learn to judge if they were new tracks or old for in this land of dryness prints might lie upon the ground for many seasons when no rain fell. In the early mornings he had to search for pebbles which carried no dew so that a hunter might know they had been turned in the night by the tread of some creature, and he had to go down on his hands and knees to seek for signs in the grass.

"Remember, boy," said Fast Foot, not once but many times, "the ground and the bush tell a story. Even on hard ground where feet leave no marks one may know in which direction a beast has gone for grass which has been knocked down always points the way the animal is going, but a pebble, dislodged by a hoof, is pushed backwards. It is the same with a snake. As it moves, it forces the sand back towards its tail. And one may even follow the track of bees. See," he would say in his great

47

anxiety to teach Garib well, and he would pick up a stone and show Garib a drop of wax so small that the boy's untrained eye had not seen it on the ground. "See, the wax fell from a bee in flight and points to the place towards which the bee is flying. Follow the drops and you will come to the tree where the bees are nesting."

Soon Garib knew the print of every bird and beast; the small hard marks of the zebra, the peculiar spoor of the hyena with its hind and fore feet of unequal size, the broad footprint of the lion.

Then he had to learn to set snares and traps and how to skin a beast and sharpen weapons. There seemed to be endless things which he must learn, and in despair Garib began to think that the day would never come when he too might twist the sinews of a beast he had killed into a bracelet to wear upon his arm.

Then at last Fast Foot said, "We shall go hunting today with the men for one of the herdsmen has brought news of rhinoceros spoor beyond the waterhole. You shall see how men hunt big game."

There was great excitement in the village, for a rhinoceros was a rare beast and its bones much prized for their fat. Armed with spears and accompanied by the dogs, the men set out in the middle of the morning, and when the sun was at its hottest, they came upon the great beast.

"It is a black rhinoceros!" Garib heard one of the men whisper in alarm. The blood was pounding through Garib's head. This was a creature so fierce that not even the lion would attack it.

"Keep close to me," whispered Fast Foot anxiously, "and do not tramp on twigs."

The men divided into two parties, one half of them approaching from the lee, the other moving cautiously to the windward side. As the wind carried the scent of the men towards their prey, the sentinel bird which sat upon its back and fed upon the insects to be found in the folds of its head and neck, flew up suddenly into the air. Instantly the black rhinoceros looked up, its small short-sighted eyes peering about angrily. At the same moment the hunters loosed the dogs, and yelping and snarling with hatred for this great creature, they rushed forward.

Snorting and tearing up the ground with its terrible horn, the rhinoceros turned and charged at the dogs. It caught one on its horn and tossed it into the air as if it had been nothing but a skin cloak. As it was preparing to charge once more the men on the leeward side ran from their cover of thorn bushes and sent a shelf of spears flying through the air into the side of the beast. In a rage the wounded animal turned upon its new assailants, but before it could reach the men, other spears were being hurled against it from behind. The rhinoceros faced about to ward off this further attack, but, once more before it could charge, the men from the leeward side hurled yet more spears.

In a frenzy of despair, tearing and ripping at the ground and bushes near it, the great creature veered from left to right, constantly kept at bay by the spears, first from one side then the other, until it was as bristling with shafts as a porcupine with quills. Finally, with a scream of pain, it charged off into the bush, sending men leaping out of its path in all directions, with its tail between its legs and the dogs biting at it from behind.

The rhinoceros did not run far. Exhausted from its wounds and the heat of the sun, it sank down helpless to the ground and the hunters closed round it to finish it off. Almost before the great beast had given its last whistling gasp the fleshers had out their sharpened knives and, with shouts and cries of triumph, were slashing at the huge grey and mud-covered mass.

After that Garib went out hunting often with Fast Foot after smaller game. When they came upon the prints of the compact-hoofed zebras, they would throw off all their clothing, even the skins about their loins which might encumber them. Then with only their bows and arrows and hunting knives they crept in stealth and silence upon the zebras, and when the leading stallion gave the alarm with a toss of its striped head and the whole herd galloped off, Garib and Fast Foot raced after them.

It was exciting work and soon Garib could run almost as

fast as Fast Foot, but, panting and elated as he always was when at last the animal lay dead at his feet, he could not help feeling a pang of disappointment. It was always Fast Foot's arrow which killed the buck or the zebra and even when the meat had been carried back to the village, Garib could not sit with the other men to eat for he had not yet been made a man. One who was still a boy might not sit with the men at the fire.

Then suddenly events began to move with greater speed. A trader arrived with more news of Haramub, and when the people heard it they went wild with excitement. True to his word, Haramub had fought yet another battle against the Cattle People and this time he had driven them right back across the Kuiseb and had become rich beyond reckoning with the Black Men's cattle. The spears and clubs of the Cattle People were of no avail against the guns of the man with two names. They were fleeing before him like buffalo before the hunters.

"*Eisey!*" screamed the men. "Soon Haramub shall drive the dogs back even from our own lands in the north. *Ai! Ai! Ai!*"

The news too seemed to have a great effect upon Arub the Big One, though, strangely, for once he spoke little of his thoughts. But he had no need to speak, for the dark kindling look in his eye and his restless pacing spoke for him.

"He is like a buck that sniffs at the green grass wind from the north and knows the new grass has sprouted and it is time to migrate," said Fast Foot, but others who were not so kind said, "The Big One is like a dog who sees a waving tail fleeing before him."

Then at last Arub the Big One stopped his pacing and called the men together.

"When I left the north I promised you that one day I would return. Now the season of waiting is over. You must prepare for war!"

"War!" echoed the men, and the women left their huts and crowded nearer anxiously.

"Yes!" shouted Arub, scowling. "War! Once the clan of Arub was a great clan. I had many people and many cattle and sheep. Now my house is growing great once more. I have many people but my herds are small. Shall I sit in my hut like a woman when there are riches to be won in the north? What this Haramub can do, I can do also! "

The men gasped, some hardly knowing what to make of such words, others, who had already guessed the cause of Arub's restlessness and shared his growing greed, beginning to smile with excitement.

"Wait! " Tomarib rose to his feet and many of the younger men frowned with impatience at the sight of his infirmity, but, old though he was, he was still the chief counsellor and must be listened to with respect. "My chief! " Tomarib's hand shook slightly as he raised it in salute, but with a visible effort he steadied it and lifted his chin with dignity. "What foolish words are these, my chief?" he asked and his voice came out so strongly that even the younger men seemed to pause and prepare to listen to the one elected by the old clan. It was as if sudden alarm for the safety of the people had once more forced Tomarib back to strength. "Why do you speak of stealing? Would you have men think Arub the Big One is a thief?"

Arub turned. His eyes blazed. "A thief! " he screamed. "You call me a thief?" And Garib who was standing listening beside the Great Hut could almost feel the words falling like blows on the old man. "Do men call Haramub a thief? Is it stealing for a man to take back what was taken from him by the Cattle People?"

But Tomarib would not be beaten down. He kept the determined set of his head and once more the people hesitated though it was obvious that they were roused by Arub's words. "My chief," he said. "I know that it is ancient law that a man may avenge the wrongs done to him, but men must use the law with wisdom. Is it wise to risk all in war when your clan is growing daily in peace?"

Now the feeling of the people seemed to swing back to Tomarib and those who were older and more moderate began to murmur in approval.

The Big One had always hated Tomarib for his ability to sway men to his thinking. Now he saw that the old man, despite his age and infirmity, still had this power which might foil his plans.

"Peace!" he thundered. "You speak of peace when honour remains unsatisfied. Are we dogs to be kicked by a black master or are we Men of Men? Answer me this, one who sat down upon the veld to die when my people were crying out with thirst and needed your counsel?"

Tomarib's weakness beside the dry pool in the desert had been forgotten for a long while, but now suddenly his past humiliation was flung upon the ground by the furious Arub and seemed to lie there naked for all to see. There was an uneasy silence.

Garib glanced quickly at Tomarib. He saw the old man flinch painfully and knew that Tomarib himself had never been able to forget his shame. Arub the Big One had dealt a master stroke and his arrow of scorn had found its mark with deadly accuracy. Garib thought Tomarib was going to fall, then the old man grasped his stick so that his knuckles showed pale under his skin and lifted his head bravely.

"I know that I have forfeited the right to speak of honour," he said, his voice quivering in spite of his effort to continue to speak strongly. "But I ask you to think as men for then your own wisdom will tell you that it is wise to live in peace." But now suddenly his dignity seemed ridiculous. It hung on him like an ill-fitting cloak and some of the men even began to laugh.

"Not peace!" shouted Arub. "War! We shall show the Cattle People what happens to those who insult the Men of Men! We shall drive them back as Haramub has done. They shall run before us like dogs and we too shall bring home great herds. We shall all be rich men, men to be respected!"

"Ai! Ai! Ai!" There were shouts from all around. "War! War! Blood must pay for blood!"

Arub the Big One listened, his sharp eyes gleaming. He turned and looked at Tomarib, but the old man was standing with his head bent. He had nothing more to say.

Flushed with triumph that he had at last defeated the counsellor who so often before had held him in check, the Big One gave a great shout. "Then it is decided," he said. "I shall walk against the Cattle People and all those who can carry the bow shall come with me. Yes, even you shall come, Tomarib," he said as if he wished to force this final humiliation on the old man to make sure of his new power.

There was a faint murmur of disapproval from some of the older men for Tomarib was too old and infirm for such a walk, and, hearing the sound, Arub snarled as if to defy anyone to speak against him. There was silence and the chief in even greater triumph shouted, "No, I shall allow no man to hide behind age!" Then suddenly his gaze fell upon Garib and he stopped. "Nor shall they hide behind youth," he said. "This son of my brother shall come also."

The people gasped. Now indeed Arub the Big One had gone too far in his cruelty. "Garib is still a boy!" they protested. "He has not yet been made a man."

"Then I shall make him a man!" screamed Arub.

And suddenly a woman's voice was raised above the rest. "Do not do this thing, my chief!" Garib saw with horror that it was his own mother. Before he could stop her she had stepped forward. "I have lost my man and now I must lose my only son. Garib is too young. Fight if you must, but leave me my child!"

Arub the Big One stared at her, fury gathering in his face that a woman dared to speak out against him. Compressing his thin lips into a scornful smile, he turned to Garib.

"Speak, boy!" he said. "Tell the people if you wish to be made a man or if you wish to remain tied to your mother's leather skirt."

Garib stood like a bird caught in a trap. For a moment his heart beat wildly with fear. He looked hastily at his mother, then back to his chief and read clearly in the narrow eyes the taunt that if he chose to remain a boy he must forever bear the stigma of one who was not fit to leave the care of women. There was no greater insult among the Men of Men than to be called *"kutsire"*, one attached to women's company. Then he dared not look again at his mother for he knew that, even without this gibe he was longing to go with the men more than anything else in the world.

"I wish to be made a man, my chief," he said loudly. "I

53

wish to go with you for it was Kahitjene of the Cattle People who killed my father."

A shout of applause ran through the crowd of men and even Arub the Big One was smiling. Garib knew that he had spoken well, but even in the dizziness of relief that washed over him he was aware of a deep hurt in his heart. But still he did not look at his mother. He had no need to feel for the mark his arrow had made upon her breast, as he had when he had shot his first bird while yet a child, to know that he had wounded her. Yet, he told himself, the ache he had felt at the sight of the dead dove so long ago had quickly passed. He had helped to kill many other creatures since then when out on the hills with Fast Foot. Indeed a man soon became used to killing.

"The boy has spoken like a true man of Arub!" cried the Big One. "It shall be as he desires." He turned to Tomarib. "And this one who is always so full of wise words shall teach him what a man must know before he may sit with other men at the fire. But teach him his wisdom quickly, old counsellor," he said, "for I mean to set out as soon as the first rains have fallen."

Five

For many days Garib lived and ate and slept in an enclosure of reeds within Tomarib's hut while the old man taught him all that it was needful for a man to know.

"In the time before men remember," Tomarib told him, "our people came from a great distance. They came from the east, travelling over the plains, their faces always turned to the setting sun until they reached the great waters of the ocean and could travel no further. And so it is, my child. All things come from the east for this is the place of the birth and the beginning. It is in the east that the sun and the moon rise, and here too the first man was made by Tsui-Goab, the Red Dawn, the Great Chief, who created the heaven and earth and causes the thunder and rain, and gives food, and skins for clothing. Tsui-Goab is the god who made all things in the dawn of the beginning."

On and on the old man talked, teaching Garib the wisdom of the Men of Men, and over and over Garib had to repeat what was said until he knew it so that he could never forget.

"And Tsui-Goab was good," Tomarib said. "In the beginning he gave every man plenty of cattle and sheep because he was very rich and he wished for all blessings to fall upon his children whom he had made. But on the earth there was a power named Gaunab, the Deceiver and the Destroyer. Gaunab sent the whirlwind to catch the spirits of men so that he could destroy the people of Tsui-Goab. And when he had grown very strong he went to war against Tsui-Goab so that he might destroy him too and be Lord of the World. He fought against Tsui-Goab and overpowered him and threw him into a pit, but Tsui-Goab rose from the pit and still lived.

Many times Gaunab overpowered Tsui-Goab but in every battle Tsui-Goab, the Great Chief, grew stronger until at last he was so big and strong that he easily conquered Gaunab. With one great blow behind the ear he knocked Gaunab into the very pit which he had dug to receive the Great Chief."

Garib listened to all with wide eyes for though he had heard the stories many times they still filled him with fear and awe for there was much in them that he did not understand.

"So, my son," said Tomarib, "as it was then, it is now and it always shall be. Tsui-Goab lives in a beautiful heaven and Gaunab lives in a dark heaven. Tsui-Goab lives in the Red Sky of dawn and Gaunab lives in the black sky. Tsui-Goab is good and Gaunab is evil and if a man wishes to live he must not allow Gaunab to catch him for Gaunab is the Destroyer and the Bringer of Death."

Garib was cramped from sitting for so long. He moved his aching legs and longed to be allowed to run across the veld once more with Fast Foot.

"My father," he said. "How is it that Tsui-Goab died many times and yet he still lived?"

Tomarib regarded him sternly. "My son," he said. "A man cannot try to understand these things for they are mysteries. He can only feel them."

"Yes, my father," said Garib. He wriggled again, but there was no escape and after a while he hardly knew what Tomarib was saying for his excited mind was already racing ahead, living a hundred brave deeds in the coming battle.

"So a man must choose to act as a man and not as a beast," the old man was telling him, "for there is that within him which gives him this knowledge. Now repeat after me these things which a man must not do. I must not light my pipe or sit down to smoke in the house of strangers until I know they are good men. I must not sit at a fire with people who have stolen cattle or cooked the meat on that fire. I must not kill without cause. I must not lie." The list was endless and many times Garib forgot the words when his attention wandered and Tomarib rebuked him sternly.

And even when Garib knew all of the law he still had to learn many other things.

"But Tsui-Goab did not leave men to struggle alone," Tomarib said. "He left the Moon and the Sun and the Thunder Cloud and all those other things which he had made to guide men. And the Moon wished to tell the Men of Men that they must not lose heart but must keep hold of their courage by looking at him."

Garib found that he was listening again. He knew what was coming for he had often heard this story told by his grandmother and wondered at its meaning when the moon was full and the people were gathered for the reed dance so that they could praise the great shining god and ask him for protection against evil.

"So the Moon called the hare and commanded him to take a message to men. 'Tell them,' he said, 'that they must watch how I rise and set and know that as I die and am renewed, so shall they die and be renewed.' But the hare forgot the words along the way and when he reached the village of men, he said, 'As I die and stay dead, so shall you die and stay dead.' On his return the Moon was so angry that he threw a stick at the hare and split open its lip. And so, my son, this is why the old people say that no man must eat the meat of the hare for he still bears upon his mouth the marks of his punishment."

Garib waited for Tomarib to explain but the old man began to get up to go and leave Garib in his seclusion to think of the day's lessons.

"But, my father," he said quickly, "does this story also have no meaning?"

Tomarib stopped and looked back. "Meanings! Meanings!" he said with an edge of impatience to his voice. Then as if he saw Garib's eagerness and look of bewilderment, his sternness faded and he said with strange gentleness. "I cannot give you the power to understand, my child, for it is only through a man's own experience of life that he may come to know the meaning of wise words. I can teach you the stories, but you must find the truth behind them for yourself, and indeed it is only through his works that a man may learn to understand any kind of wisdom."

He regarded Garib steadily, then seeing that he was still confused, he came back and sat down. "I shall try to explain,"

57

he said kindly. "For me, my son, the words of the Moon have this meaning, for this is what my deeds have taught me. They tell me to have courage, for though I have been destroyed by Arub the Big One so that I may never again be respected as a counsellor, I may yet live and be of use. I have found this out through my work of teaching you."

Garib looked up in surprise and, seeing Tomarib's old toothless mouth working as if it were chewing on grass, he was suddenly filled with pity. Indeed Tomarib had spoken truly when he had said that he had been destroyed by the Big One, for surely only a broken man could clutch at such a straw of comfort! Could any man be satisfied to be nothing more than a teller of stories? Why, even a woman could be this!

But, unaware of Garib's thoughts, Tomarib was speaking again in the same solemn voice. "And the message of the Moon is true, my child. Every evening a man dies and is covered by the darkness of night, yet at each dawn he is renewed, and if he turns his eyes towards the east, towards the beginning of all things, he may see the Red Sky of Tsui-Goab triumphant in the Dawn and know that Good is still the conqueror of Evil."

Then he looked at Garib and saw the pity in the boy's eyes. He sighed softly and stood up once more. "It is no use," he said. "You cannot understand. I see that the cruelty of Arub the Big One wishes to make a man and warrior of you before you are ready. It is not easy to be a man. But have patience, boy," he added, "for you will discover many things which you do not believe now. And when you look at the Moon know that it tells the story of the life of man. First the Moon is young. Then he grows and becomes great. Then he begins to grow small again as he wanes so that he may learn wisdom. And then the Moon dies and disappears from the sky and the night is black. Who can tell what wonders may lie in that darkness of death through which the Moon must travel so that he may be renewed and born again? So think on these things, Garib, son of Arub the Hunter, for I have given you all the words I know and you must now go out into the world to seek along many roads for their meaning, for until you find it you shall not know even that you are a man."

He walked to the door. "So think well," he said, "for I go now to tell Arub that you are ready for the priest."

But when the old man had gone Garib did not give one thought to the Moon or even to Tsui-Goab. He was to be made a man. He was to leave forever the safe country of boyhood.

And the very next morning the men came and dragged him from Tomarib's hut. They tore the old skin garments from his loins and brought him naked to kneel before the men of the clan. And then Arub the Big One was shouting out his name and asking the men if they found him fitting to sit with them at the fire, and Tomarib was telling him that he was released from the care of his mother and must no longer eat with the women or do any of those things which a man must not do or he would be cast out from the company of men.

Then suddenly the priest was beside him. Garib stared with terror at the sharp piece of quartz in the priest's hand, but his fear of being cast out from manhood was even greater than his terror of the knife and he did not try to run away. He lay down upon the ground and bit his lip to keep from screaming as the quartz cut seven long shallow gashes on his breast and ash was rubbed into the wounds to staunch the blood.

"Garib, son of the Hunter!" the Big One was shouting. "I give you your Great Name, Arub, for you are now Garib Arub, *doro-aob*, a man among the Men of Men!"

After that Garib was given new clothes and led to the circle of men so that he could take his place and drink with them and share with them the meat of the sacrifice as a man.

And even after that there was no time to think for at the feast Arub told them that his spies had returned, bringing news that rain had fallen to the north and there was water to be found in the Land of Sand and Stones and that the warriors were to set out at dawn.

With his quiver of arrows on his back and his bow hanging from his shoulder, Garib went to say goodbye to his mother.

She stared at him and said nothing.

Garib looked down to hide the uncertainty in his eyes. Was

he a boy, or was he a man, or was he lost in some frightening land in between? In his excitement and confusion Garib did not know and suddenly, in spite of his warrior's weapons, he felt like a small child who wishes for a caress of love so that he may feel safe. He knew then that some part of what Tomarib had said was true. It was not easy to be a man.

"Do not grieve, *Mames*," he said, trying to sound bold. "See, the priest has given me a charm of wood to wear upon my breast to protect me from harm and he has burnt the heart of a crow and scattered it to the winds so that our enemy shall be scattered and we shall be triumphant. You shall not lose me, *Mames*."

His mother looked at him. She touched his face quickly and her eyes filled with tears, but still she said nothing. It was as if she knew that she had lost her son already.

Six

The men of Arub walked for many days. They crossed the
Land of Sand and Stone, going further and further north,
stopping only to hunt for meat and to camp at night. And all
the way they remained great in courage, and though Tomarib
tried to warn them that too much confidence might turn
warriors into fools, they did not pay the slightest heed to his
words of caution. And after a while the old man ceased to
speak, for his strength was gone and in exhaustion he plodded
on in silence.

Boasting and shouting of all that they would do when they
reached the hated Cattle People, they passed close to the Hills
of the Killing of the Elephant, and at last after two more days
of walking Arub's spies came running back to the camp to say
that they had found a village belonging to the Black Men.

And so eager was the Big One for battle that he would not
even wait so that the tired warriors could rest. "What Haramub can do, I can do also!" he shouted, and on the very next
day before dawn he led his warriors to the top of the low hill
that hid the village from view.

There on the plain below amid tall thorn trees and silver-
grey scrub, were the houses of the Cattle People. Inside a large
circular fence of thorn bush stood the huts, domed and plas-
tered with mud and cow dung in a fashion strange to the Nama
eye, arranged in order along the edge of a cross-shaped piece
of ground. Within the fence too were the cattle enclosures,
still filled at this early time of day with beasts which even
from a distance appeared fine and fat and many in number.
Thin clouds of blue-white smoke were rising from the holes
in the tops of some of the roofs and hung on the soft dawn

air in a drifting haze over the plain, but the doors of most of the huts were still closed.

In wonder and curiosity Garib stared down at the village. In his confusion he had begun to think that no such people as the Black Men really existed and that the planned battle would take place only in a dream. Had he not lived through it already many times in glorious dreams? Now the strange huts lay before them and suddenly no one was boasting.

"Which people are these?" whispered Fast Foot, peering out with the others from behind the stones on the hill. "What is their name?" But no one could answer, and then Garib knew why Tomarib had spoken out against the raid. These were not the people who had harmed the clan of Arub. The Big One was only going against them because he was greedy for their cattle.

With a heart pounding so loudly with fear that he hardly knew even what was happening, Garib watched one of the scouts making his cautious way towards the high thorn fence that surrounded the village. He could hardly be seen against the ochre-coloured earth. Then after what seemed a long time there came the signal the men had been waiting for—three short blasts on the springbok horn.

And suddenly the hill was alive with warriors as Arub the Big One and his men raced down the slope and across the plain. And at the same moment the dogs in the village began to bark wildly. Hut doors were thrown open. There were shouts of alarm. People were running.

The Big One had hoped to take the village by surprise but as the Men of Men neared the gates the tall Black Men came streaming out to defend their homes. Arub's warriors halted. Bows twanged and arrows went winging through the air. Garib stared in wild disbelief as he saw the man beside him fall with a feathered shaft quivering in his chest.

For how long the two sides shot at each other from a distance Garib did not know. He was aware only of himself and of the drumming of the blood in his head and the shaking of his hands as he struggled to draw his arrows from his quiver. He hardly saw even where he was aiming. Everything seemed blurred by his own fear.

Then the arrows were finished. The men threw away their bows and tossed off their empty quivers and took up their spears.

"Kill them!" screamed Arub the Big One, but Garib hardly heard him.

But before the men could form into their ranks for the final charge the Black Men were running, and they were not running away in terror as Arub had promised. They were thundering across the plain towards the little Men of Men. Garib looked up in horror and consternation, and in the sudden shock he saw them with awful clarity. The Cattle People were all that the travellers had said they were. They were half as tall again as the men of the Nama nation. Their skins were as black as night, their hair long and twisted into black cords that leapt around their heads as they ran. In their right hands they carried great knobbed clubs and in their left equally great broad-bladed spears and, half naked though they were, they were a terrible sight.

"Run!" someone was shouting. "Run, Garib!"

Garib thought it was the voice of Fast Foot but though he could hear the words and understand them it was as if his terror had turned him into stone. He saw that the Men of Men were running in all directions. Arub the Big One was bounding over bushes as he fled towards the shelter of the hill and all those who were in front of Garib were rushing past him in disorder.

"Garib! Garib! Run for the battle is over!" shouted Fast Foot above the tumult, but Garib still could not move. He could only stare at the Cattle People as they poured like a flood across the veld. As they reached the fleeing Men of Men they began to lay about them with their clubs. Spears flashed and turned in the bright early light. The men of Arub were screaming and falling everywhere.

A hand grabbed Garib's arm and jerked him backwards. "Come, Young One!" cried Fast Foot in despair.

And then all at once it was too late to flee. The Cattle People were upon Garib and Fast Foot. Garib saw the short heavy club raised in the air. It was smooth and made of dark red wood. Then Garib closed his eyes and the next moment

63

a blinding pain struck him and he went spinning down into a bottomless pit of darkness.

"So you are awake at last," said a voice out of the darkness.

Garib tried to open his eyes. His head ached and he felt a great heaviness in his limbs. He lay still, wishing rather to drift back into sleep for he was aware of a deep dread and he did not wish to discover what it was. But the voice would not let him alone.

"Garib!" it whispered urgently. "Do you hear me?"

Garib opened his eyes. Fast Foot was bending over him, his big face wrinkled with anxiety and concern. "Are you all right, Young One?"

Slowly and painfully Garib looked past Fast Foot. He saw that he was in a hut, but not the kind of hut he knew. The floor was hard and smelt strange.

"Where are we?" he asked dully.

"We are in the hut of the Cattle People," whispered Fast Foot. "Do you not remember, Garib? See, there is a great lump on your head where they hit you. We have been captured by the Black Men."

Garib stared up at him and could no longer keep from remembering. He remembered the awful charge of the Cattle People and the slaughter and his childish terror.

"Did they catch you, Fast Foot, because you stayed behind with me?" he asked.

As if Fast Foot guessed at his thoughts, he patted Garib's arm quickly. "*Ai!* Do not think of the battle. You were too young for such sights. You were too young. And it is not so bad, Young One. At least we are alive. Tomarib and many of the others were killed and the Big One has fled. It was indeed a foolish raid as the old counsellor said."

But Garib continued to stare up at Fast Foot. "What will the Cattle People do with us?"

"*Ai!*" said Fast Foot, and then even he looked away. "I have been speaking to one of their servants, a man from the nation of the Mountain People who speaks our language, and he says that we are to be kept as herdsmen and slaves."

Seven

The hut in which Garib and Fast Foot found themselves was, they soon discovered, the servants' hut, and in the evening the little black men of the nation of the Mountain People who were servants to their tall masters, returned. Garib stared at them as they crowded into the dark hut. They were thin almost to emaciation, and on their backs were many scars, and when a dish of food was thrust in through the low doorway they fought fiercely like animals over the thick sour milk.

Neither Garib nor Fast Foot was surprised at the wretched appearance of the bondsmen. Nor did they feel any indignation when they discovered that no fire was lit in the servants' hut at night nor any sheepskin blanket or cover given to the men to keep out the cold. Servants in Arub's village had received no better treatment. Those who were captured or sought protection from their enemies by becoming bondsmen to others knew to expect nothing more than a place to build a hut and an occasional dish of food in time of plenty in return for the services they rendered their masters. This was the lot of enslaved peoples and Fast Foot seemed able to accept it with resignation. In his hunger he even snatched up a boiled root which had fallen to the dirty earth floor unnoticed by the Mountain People.

And after a while he began to answer the questions of the other bondsmen and to ask questions in return, but Garib crouched against the wall, hardly listening, lost in misery. ·

"Escape?" he heard one servant reply to some question of Fast Foot's. "No, master, such thoughts are foolishness. We too were captured by the Cattle People and those who tried to run away were soon caught and killed."

The Mountain Man had called Fast Foot "master" for the Men of Men had always felt superior to all others. And now Garib and Fast Foot were nothing but slaves, doomed forever, without hope of escape, to be starved and beaten by people whom Arub the Big One had scorned as no better than dogs. Could there be any fate worse than this? Garib rested his aching head against the hut wall. He could not bear to think of it.

And later when the servants settled down to sleep, cold as he was, he could not force himself to move closer to the other men for warmth. Shivering and ill, he sat hugging his knees as if he wished to creep into himself and shut out all else, and he thought with bitterness of the words of the old soothsayer. Surely it had been a cruel joke to tell him he would walk the road to glory.

The next morning, light-headed from hunger and from the wound on his head, Garib followed one of the bondsmen to the hut of the man who was to be his master while Fast Foot was taken to a different hut to start his work. He listened dumbly as the little Mountain Man told him what to do. He was to fill the waterpots from the waterhole below the village, and collect firewood, and sweep the floor like a woman. And when he was not busy in the village he was to help with the herding and watering of the cattle. But Garib hardly understood what was being said even though the bondsman spoke a rough form of the Nama language. He gazed at the Black Man with the arrogant features who was his new master, then stared stupidly about him like one who had lost his senses.

All around the people of the village had gathered to see the new slaves and Garib saw that the Black Men were very different from the Men of Men. They were so tall, their faces so long, their noses so slender and their eyes so contemptuous. And though the men wore little but a skin apron kept in place by an endless length of leather thong wound round and round the hips, the women were decked out in more finery than he had ever seen upon a person. They had long skirts, hanging at the back to their knees and lifting in front to show pleated under-dresses of skins. Round their hips were wide white belts of ostrich egg shell beads, across their shoulders hung long cloaks, and on their heads were elaborately-made hats of stiffened hide, rising in three points like long ears, and on their feet were pointed sandals, bigger than those which the Men of Men sometimes wore. In addition to all this, they seemed covered with ornaments and beads. Heavy chains of small iron balls hung from their necks and hips and arms, more strings hung down their backs from their caps, and yet more coils of iron beads were tied around the lower part of the leg in such numbers that the lowest rings dragged upon the ground. And some of the men and women, especially those with the most ornaments and whom Garib judged to be the richest, were so besmeared with grease and red ochre that even their clothing and beads shone with a bright sharp red in the sunlight.

He saw also that the two front upper teeth of the people had been chipped to make the shape of a small arrowhead pointing upwards so that it gave their speech a soft lisping sound. They were indeed a very strange and frightening people.

Then, fearful lest Garib's staring angered the Cattle People, the bondsman thrust a waterpot into Garib's hand and told him to come to the fountain, and with the same stupid look Garib followed him. His servitude had begun.

For two days Garib would not speak, even to Fast Foot. Nor did he eat, for the bondsmen fought savagely over the few scraps that were given them and the dish was soon empty. Then on the afternoon of the second day Fast Foot came to him while he was sitting dejectedly on a stone near his master's cattle.

"Young One," he said. "I have brought you some gum to eat. Take it. Take it." He pushed a large cake of gum into Garib's hand. "You must not sit like this. There is plenty of gum to be found. See, how it oozes down from the black thorn trees into the sand. We must do as the other slaves do, Garib. We must find our own food and care for ourselves. You must make a digging stick so that you can dig for roots and veld food. We must do these things, Young One," he added earnestly, "so that we may live."

Garib looked down at the cake in his hand. He had often

eaten gum while yet a child on the veld. Then to please Fast Foot who was gazing at him so anxiously, he lifted the food and bit into it. It was crisp and tasteless, but as he chewed upon it a little strength seemed to come back into his body. He took another mouthful and another until the whole cake was finished.

And on his way back to the village with the cattle that night he picked up a sturdy stick which he saw lying in the sand. That night he sharpened it with a flake of stone and the next morning hardened it, when no one was looking, in the fire outside his master's hut. When he went out herding later, he took the stick with him and when he saw the thick green shoots of a veld onion showing beside a tuft of white grass near the path, he stopped. The stick cut strongly and sharply into the hard earth beside the bulb. It was a good stick which he had made and Garib felt a small stirring of pride. It was like the first red bud swelling upon the drought-blackened branches of a thorn tree. He thought fleetingly of Tomarib's words of wisdom, that life might come from death through the work of a man's hands, but he still could not comprehend the meaning, for to Garib the life of a slave could never be life, only continuing death.

But, without realizing it, he began to look around him and, though he still felt little interest in anything, he learnt that his master's name was Kamoja and that he was the chief among the men of the village, and he soon discovered too that it was better for him to do his work with energy for then he received fewer blows from Kamoja's club upon his shoulders.

And then, strangely, it was Garib who was adapting more quickly than Fast Foot. It was as if the very depth of his despair now, like the rebound from a dive into a deep pool, was thrusting him upward. Or perhaps it was because he was younger and quicker in mind than the hunter and not even slavery would quite suppress his eagerness for life. Though he still would not eat from the servants' dish or have much to do with the other bondsmen, it became a matter of pride with him that he should keep himself alive on the foods he could gather with his own hands from the veld. And in a little while he was beginning to know words in the Black Men's language and he

68

was able to explain many things to Fast Foot who still could understand nothing of what the Cattle People were saying.

"*Ai!*" he said. "These people talk of nothing but cattle!" There was contempt in his voice for he liked to speak of his masters with scorn to ease the pain of humiliation in his heart. "Even their songs are all about oxen! Possessing so many cattle has made them more stupid even than baboons. And, Fast Foot," he added with a laugh, "do you know what they say? They say that all men and beasts were made by their god Ndjambi and came out of an Omumborombonga tree in the north. They do not even know that it was Tsui-Goab, the Great Creator, who made all men."

Fast Foot listened in amazement, his eyes filled with admiration for Garib's cleverness.

"And this Ndjambi's power lies in Kamoja's fire outside his hut where the men sit. Each night Kamoja's chief wife carries a burning log into her hut to keep the flame alive till morning. The fire belongs to their ancestors and may never be extinguished. It is this fire, Kamoja says, which gave them power to conquer us!"

But as the moons passed and there seemed no hope of ever escaping from Kamoja's village, Garib began to forget some of his bitterness and he saw that, though there were many differences between the Men of Men and the Cattle People, there was much that was the same also. The Black Men liked to dance and sing and feast as much as the people of Arub, and in some ways, though Garib would not have admitted it, they seemed even better. Their appearance was very fine and they always walked with slowness and dignity with their heads held high. And were they not kinder to their dogs so that few starving curs were to be seen about the village? Their children too they seemed to love, the women greasing their babies daily and gently stretching out their limbs so that they might grow straight, and even the arrogant Kamoja petted his daughters and called them "little onions" in play.

Then early one morning when Garib had lived as a slave with the Cattle People for two summers Fast Foot came running to the trees where Garib was gathering wood for his master's fire.

69

"Garib!" he whispered. He was almost trembling with agitation.

Garib stopped in the act of breaking a branch from a thorn tree. "What is it, Fast Foot?" he asked.

"Come! Come!"

Garib left his wood and ran after Fast Foot as he had in the days when Fast Foot had taught him to hunt. They went over the plain until they came to the slope leading down to the river. The whole of Kamoja's village seemed to be there already, looking down into the dry river bed, and when they came nearer Garib saw the reason. The way was filled with oxen. And the oxen were not in files of one or two. They covered the whole bed and banks of the river with one living mass of cattle as far as Garib could see.

"Whose cattle are they?" asked Garib in amazement. Never in all his life had he seen such numbers.

Fast Foot turned to look at him, his forehead wrinkling in bewilderment. "I saw the people running and came to see what sight drew them," he said. "The bondsmen say these many thousands of beasts belong to Kahitjene!"

"Kahitjene! The man who killed my father! The man who drove us from our home!" Garib had never heard any more about Kahitjene than Arub the Hunter had been able to tell before his death. He felt a sudden shock. It was as if a cold hand had descended upon his shoulder.

"*Eisey!*" he said and his voice trembled slightly. "I did not know this Kahitjene was so rich and powerful."

"The bondsmen tell me he is the richest Cattle King in the whole land of the Cattle People."

Garib stared down at the endless stream of oxen. "Is Kahitjene here with his cattle also?" he whispered.

"No," said Fast Foot, "he is not here. His house is further to the north. These droves are only a part of his great herds. He has so many cattle they cannot all graze in one place. These have been in the care of some of his kinsmen to the east, but now he has sent word that the herds must be brought across the river so that they may be safe from Haramub."

Garib gaped at Fast Foot a second time. First Kahitjene, now Haramub. In his servitude Garib had almost forgotten

70

that two such men existed. His slavery had been like a bank on to which he had been washed by a flood at the time of the great storms which in a few moments could turn a dry river bed into a raging torrent, and he had lain there, scarcely alive, for two summers. Now suddenly he saw the wall of water once more rushing down upon him to carry him back into the river of life and, like a man who is not sure that he can swim, he was very afraid.

Fast Foot looked round cautiously to make sure none of Kamoja's people who were gathered higher up the river could hear. "The bondsmen say that Haramub is sweeping the land to the south. They say he is coming this way!"

Garib could hardly grasp so much at once. "Kahitjene," he breathed. "And Haramub." Then the full meaning of the news reached him. If Haramub were sweeping the country he would not leave Kamoja's prosperous village untouched. But where was he now? Was he far or near? Garib could hardly breathe with the sudden excitement.

"Come, Garib," said Fast Foot, pulling him away. "We shall be beaten for leaving our work."

When they returned to the village they found all in confusion. The head drover of Kahitjene's cattle was already seated outside Kamoja's hut drinking beer and telling the news.

"We defeated these small men before," Kamoja was shouting. "If they dare to attack us we shall defeat them again. They are nothing but dogs that yap at the heels of their masters!"

And they need not have feared a beating. None of the men had any thoughts to spare for firewood or erring slaves. They had no time even to be impressed by Kahitjene's great herds that continued to pass close to the village along the dry river bed in such numbers that the last of the droves only disappeared into the distance on the evening of the second day, leaving the banks on either side of the river denuded of grass or any green thing as if locusts had passed that way. Everywhere men were sharpening and polishing their spears until they glittered as the men turned them in the sunlight, and preparing their finery and testing their bows.

With mounting excitement Garib watched them. "Haramub is coming! Haramub is coming!" he kept saying to himself and he remembered the promise the little chief had made to him so long ago. "I shall remember you for I see that you are a boy of spirit. Come to me again when you are a man for I may indeed have need of you."

But when at last all was ready and the men stood dressed in their war clothes with their weapons about them, Garib could only stare. These men who were gathering to dance the war dance were not the half-naked men Arub the Big One had surprised at dawn. These were warriors in all the strength of their finery with ostrich feathers waving above their dark brows. Over their shoulders they wore karosses of lion and leopard skin, on their feet long pointed sandals, and around their necks and arms iron rings and beads. On their backs were their skin quivers full of poisoned arrows, in their hands their bows and great stabbing spears, and in the thick coiled girdle around their hips were several large-headed clubs, ready to be unsheathed in an instant, each one capable of smashing a man's skull with a single blow. As Garib watched them beginning the dance, their strong limbs gleaming with grease and red ochre as they stamped and twisted and waved their oxtail-plumed spears, and heard them boasting of their strength in war, he felt uncertain stirrings of doubt.

And when he heard their priest shouting to the spirits of the ancestors behind the thorn fence which separated the place of the sacred fire from the rest of the village, he could no longer feel scorn for the Black Men. What magic might there not lie in the holy firesticks of the ancestors of Kamoja which Garib had seen carried from the Great Hut? What power in this god Ndjambi?

All the time scouts were returning to the village to tell their chief of the progress of the Warlike People, and when at length one of them came rushing to Kamoja shouting that the enemy had camped for the night behind the hill, the Cattle People tied Garib and Fast Foot with long thongs to the centre post of the servants' hut so that they could not join the horsemen who were their kinsmen.

"*Ai!*" whispered Garib. "Surely even Haramub with all his

72

guns cannot triumph against such a people."

The people of Haramub attacked just after dawn. The sound of the gunfire thundered and crashed from the direction of the hill behind the village. It echoed and re-echoed against the iron-stone rocks and even though Garib had heard the noise of the little chief's gun when he had shot the parrot in the tree beside the village of Arub the Big One, he was not prepared for the sudden and terrifying sound made by many weapons firing together. He gazed wide-eyed into the darkness of the hut roof. Beside him he could feel Fast Foot shivering with fright.

They were alone in the hut for the other bondsmen were out helping their masters and the door was closed. They could see nothing and had no way of knowing how the battle was going. Somewhere nearby they could hear women and children screaming with fear. Then there was the sound of heavy feet running so that the floor of the hut trembled, and the dull clatter of the iron beads the warriors wore upon their legs. And all the while the guns were firing and echoing and firing again till Garib's ears were deaf with the vibration. The noise and the shouting and confusion went on for some time, then it lessened and the firing ceased. In the distance Garib and Fast Foot could hear men calling but they could not make out the words.

Then suddenly there was a shout outside the servants' hut and the next moment the door was torn from the entrance, letting in the light.

"What treasure do the dogs store in this place that they keep it shut?" a loud voice demanded in the language of the Men of Men, and before Garib could think what was happening, a man, dressed in the leather trousers of Haramub's people, was standing in the hut, frowning as if he could not see properly in the dimness.

Garib hardly dared to believe his eyes. Could it really be true that Haramub had defeated Kamoja and he and Fast Foot were free? In confusion and astonishment he saw that the big rough-faced man was holding strings of iron beads in both hands, and across his shoulders was the leopard skin

73

kaross which had been worn by Kamoja himself. It was still dripping with blood. And he knew then that it was indeed true for this man of Haramub had been gathering up all the wealth he could find in the village as his prize in victory.

Garib tried to shout but in his emotion his voice broke and his words were no more than a croak. "We are here!"

The man whipped round. He saw Garib and Fast Foot tied to the pole and stared in amazement.

"*Ai!*" he shouted to someone outside. "Hendrick, come and see what I have found!"

At once a smaller mean-faced man joined him. "*Eisey*, my Kaptein," Hendrick exclaimed in a shrill high-pitched voice. "It is two men of the Nama nation. Two Nama men tied to a pole!" But after the first astonished glance he seemed to lose interest in Garib and Fast Foot. His arms too were laden with loot from the village and his small eyes roved restlessly round the hut as if in search of more.

"How did you come to be here?" asked the bigger man who had been called *Kaptein*.

Garib did not know what the foreign word meant but he realized it must be some title of authority for the man had the air of one accustomed to command. Garib looked quickly at Fast Foot but saw that he was still too bewildered to answer.

"We were caught by the Cattle People, *khub*," he said. "We have been living in this village as slaves for two summers."

"Slaves!" exclaimed the Kaptein, and suddenly he gave a loud hoot of laughter. "*Ai*, Hendrick!" he said to the smaller man, "I came looking for treasure in this hut and all I found was slaves!" And with a swamping feeling of dismay Garib realized what he and Fast Foot must look like to Haramub's two soldiers. What a sorry sight they must be with their skins ungreased, the leather of their loin cloths hanging in blackened tatters from their hips, and the scars of many beatings showing even in this dim light upon their shoulders.

Hendrick moved impatiently. "Come, my Kaptein," he said, whining slightly. "This is only the servants' hut. There is nothing here. Leave the pieces of rubbish for it is almost time to go and there is still much wealth to collect."

In shock Garib stared up at them, dismay turning quickly

74

to horror. What was the man saying? Leave him and Fast Foot tied to the post to die of starvation in what must now be an empty village? Could any men be so low in their nature as to do such a thing? The long thong with which he was bound was cutting into his wrists and his arms and shoulders ached with cramp. "We are not pieces of rubbish!" he cried in alarm. "We belong to the people of Arub the Big One."

"Arub the Big One?" The Kaptein grinned. He turned to Hendrick. "*Ai!* Do you remember Arub the Big One, Hendrick? He was that loud-mouthed idiot whose house was like the village of a Bushman."

Garib felt his throat closing so that he could scarcely breathe, but at the same time his horror was turning quickly to anger. "Arub the Big One gave your master Haramub food and honey beer when he passed by our village!" he cried out hotly.

"Hush, Young One," whispered Fast Foot in alarm. "These are important men."

The Kaptein heard him and began to laugh again. "*Ai,*" he said. "The one with the thin legs speaks truly. The people of Haramub are important people, and I am not surprised that this Arub gave us food. If he had been foolish enough to refuse, his bush village might well have looked as Kamoja's house looks now, and you, boy, would not have lived to speak impudently to Haramub's Kaptein."

Tears sprang unbidden to Garib's eyes and he pushed Fast Foot away angrily. "I am not a boy! I am a man!" he said. "And I know your master. Take me to him and you will see that we are his friends."

"*Eisey!*" said the Kaptein, pretending to be surprised at this bold speech. "So you are a man and a friend of the chief. Indeed you must be important also. But I cannot take you to Haramub for he is not here. Did you imagine that he would have come himself to defeat so insignificant a people as the tribe of Kamoja?"

In utter confusion Garib gazed up at the big man. He had thought the warriors of Kamoja so powerful that no one could overcome them. Yet Haramub had thought so little of them that he had not even come himself.

75

"But do not despair, Young One. We will not leave you here," said the Kaptein. He was grinning again mockingly, but his big rough face wore an expression which was not so unfeeling as that of the smaller man and there was a glint of humour in his eyes. He put down the bracelets of iron beads he was carrying and bent to cut through the prisoner's bonds. "The one you call Haramub is not far distant and we are going now to his village at Niais. Kamoja and his men are all dead, but you and Thin Legs can walk with the women and children we have captured and then you will be able to meet the chief and speak to him yourself."

Eight

For three days Haramub's men travelled to the east. In front went the Kaptein and his horsemen, behind them Garib and Fast Foot and the captured people, and last of all the large herds of Kamoja's cattle driven by drovers on horseback.

When they camped for the night they made huge fires and the people slept in a close circle around them and left the cattle to gather about them and make a barrier against the wild beasts for, as one of the drovers told Garib, this was a country sharp for lions.

After a while they came out on to a wide plain covered with grey-green trees and brown bushy scrub and large ant-heaps that rose up out of the red soil. They crossed many dry river beds and at last reached the place where Haramub had made his home.

All along the way Garib had tried to hold on to the belief that everything would be all right when they came to Haramub, that somehow the little man from the south would end their bondage and also the disdain which his men still showed towards him and Fast Foot even though their master Kamoja was dead.

But the more he came to know the men on the journey, the more he realized that they were not the same people he remembered who had been glad enough to share food and drink with Arub the Big One. The Warlike People now had about them a confidence and an arrogance which could not be matched even by the Cattle People. They had grown so powerful through their victories that few men, even in secret, would now dare to call them "wearers of hats".

And when at last Garib stood on the bank of the river

beside Haramub's village, he could only gaze about him in awe. To the north and north-east were high mountains rising one behind the other till the highest and furthest peaks showed blue-grey in the distance, and within the arc of hills was a wide plain covered with the huts of Haramub's people in groups of five or six together, with sheep and cattle enclosures beside them, and in between the groups of round mat houses of the Men of Men were the small conical bush huts of their Mountain People servants. Indeed Haramub was no longer a homeless wanderer. His home was finer by far even than that of Games the queen as Garib could remember it.

When the people in the village heard the shouts of the returning warriors, they came rushing towards them in their hundreds, men, women and children, and even the servants, all jostling and pushing and screaming with excitement, each one trying to reach up and touch the bodies of the men and exclaiming over the rich strings of beads and other treasure that they were carrying.

Giving their horses over to their servants, the men went with the Kaptein up the broad well-trodden path to what Garib knew must be Haramub's hut for it was bigger and finer than all the others, and Garib and Fast Foot, not knowing what else to do, followed behind with the captives.

A respectful hush fell over the crowd outside the chief's hut. Anxiously and eagerly Garib strained to see over the shoulders of the men in front of him. He saw that Haramub, looking much the same in his smallness and slimness, had come out and was standing near to his door, attended by several of the elders of the town.

The Kaptein was standing in front of Haramub, obviously telling of the success of the raid, but they were speaking in the foreign language of the south which the men sometimes used, and Garib could not understand what they were saying. The Kaptein pointed towards the cattle and the frightened crowd of captives and Haramub's gaze moved over them with calm satisfaction.

Then suddenly, before Garib was prepared for it, the Kaptein was beckoning to him and Fast Foot and the men were pushing them forward. The Kaptein spoke quickly, pointing.

The little chief glanced first at Fast Foot. He showed no interest. "You are the men of Arub the Big One?" he asked.

"Yes, yes, *khub*," said Fast Foot hurriedly. "That is so."

Then Haramub turned to Garib. It was the same steady gaze Garib remembered. The stare of a leopard. The little chief looked at him. A slightly puzzled expression came into his eyes and Garib's heart beat wildly with expectation. Haramub's gaze lingered on Garib a moment longer, then he turned back to the Kaptein.

Garib was sure Haramub had recognized him, sure he would now ask his name. He listened in a fever of impatience as the little chief spoke. "I remember Arub the Big One," Haramub said. "I had heard that he was defeated by Kamoja and that his clan had become weak and scattered as a result. They are no longer at the waterhole on the southern plains. I cannot say where they are. But these Namas make good herdsmen and I have need of more helpers. Give them food and a hut for I shall allow them to stay here with me."

Then, as if he had more important matters to attend to, he turned to his elders, and then, without so much as another glance at Garib, he was walking away towards the river to divide out the captured herds.

"*Eisey!*" whispered Fast Foot. "The great chief did not forget the Big One," he said as if this filled him with wonder. "And he allows us to stay in his house! Indeed the stars that shine upon us from heaven have been kind to us, Young One, for we could not travel alone across the desert to search for our lost people."

But Garib was staring after Haramub in anguish and dismay. He had been so sure the chief had recognized him. He opened his mouth as if, now that Haramub was gone and the opportunity lost, the words he had planned to say to remind the little chief of his promise, were straining to pour out.

The next moment he and Fast Foot were swallowed up again into the triumphant throng following after Haramub. They were jostled along by the mob, pushed and shoved even by the Mountain People servants.

Then when the cattle had been shared out a grand reed dance began to celebrate Haramub's victory over the Cattle

People. As the wild gay strains of the pipe music were heard from the clearing near the Great Hut, people came running from all directions, the men bringing their flutes and the women all the finery they had been able to snatch up. The men formed an immense ring in the centre of the clearing, and with bodies bowed and pipes to their lips, began to hop up and down with bent knees, moving jerkily and slowly round the ring in time to the rhythm. Then the women, singing in loud shrill voices, started to clap their hands and to dance with small shuffling steps round the men, with their hips thrust out backwards and their bodies twisting.

The dancing grew wilder and wilder. The men leapt into the air and in growing ecstasy threw their bodies into every contortion, striking the soles of their feet together, and the women whirled round so that the large skin karosses from their shoulders billowed out behind them. The clearing was filled with such noise and dust that it seemed the whole town of Niais had been caught in a frenzy of madness.

Ai! thought Garib. Disappointment was like a bitter pain inside him. Surely his own madness had been as great as that of the dancers when he had allowed himself to begin to dream again of glory! With a burning feeling of shame, Garib thought of how close he had come to boasting of Haramub's promise to him. How young and foolish he had shown himself to be to have imagined, even for one moment, that so great a chief as Haramub had become would trouble himself to remember a mere boy he had seen once in the home of so insignificant a man as Arub the Big One.

After the dance Garib and Fast Foot were shown to a comfortable hut where they might live with men from other tribes of the Nama nation who had left their homes and come to join Haramub so that they might seek their fortune. And the next day they began their work as cattle herds, going each morning to the enclosure of the village where they helped to break in untrained beasts to become useful as pack-oxen.

Garib did not dislike the work. He enjoyed the noise and the excitement when one of the wild oxen was caught around its leg with a looped thong and the herdsmen rushed in to

80

help secure the kicking, bellowing beast and to tumble it, amid much shouting and yelling, into the dust so that its nose could be pierced for the nose-stick and its training with sand-bags could begin. And Garib soon discovered that he had an aptitude for handling cattle and did not have to use fire as some of the other men did to force an ox, unused to the pack, to move. He found that he could coax the stubborn beasts to obey in a way that was more effective than all the beating and yelling of some of the other herdsmen.

Nor could he say that he was ill-treated or starved as he had so often been in the house of Kamoja. There was always plenty to eat even though the food was not what Garib had been accustomed to in his own home. Zebra and buck seldom found their way into the pots of the Warlike People. Hara-mub had cleared the country of game for a great distance all round Niais with his guns, but no one went hungry for there seemed to be an endless supply of captured cattle. And these cattle were not kept for feast days and sacrifice as was the custom among the men of the Nama nation who could not squander their wealth with impunity. They were slaughtered daily in great numbers as food for the village.

"The Cattle People still possess many herds for us to gather," one of the men told Garib when he expressed surprise.

But as the days passed Garib saw more and more that these Warlike People were almost as different from the men of Arub as the Cattle People. Not only did they have many horses and peculiar clothing and terrifying weapons and often spoke a strange language, but, instead of the rough earthen pots of the Namas, they cooked their food in large black iron ones which they had brought from the south, and, instead of bowls and dishes of clay and wood, they had vessels of an unknown painted metal that clanked and clattered as the women washed them in the river. And more wonderful even than this, the men of Haramub sometimes washed themselves! What Nama would have dared to use water upon his body to cleanse him-self for fear of washing away his powers of hunting? Yet so powerful and clever were the people in Niais that they not only washed themselves but sometimes even washed their clothing in their metal pails outside their huts.

Their names too were strange and wonderful. Though most of them had names known to and used by the Nama people, they also called each other Jacob and Daniel and Solomon and many other words which Garib could not understand.

The Kaptein, whose name Garib soon learnt was Pieter, explained where these words came from. "*Ai!* man of Arub," he said with a mocking gleam in his eye. "Some of the names we received from our Dutch masters in the Cape. Others came from the White Man's Book which tells him about God. But then you have never heard about God, have you, Garib?"

Garib flushed. "I have heard of our god," he said, speaking out bravely. "Tomarib, the old counsellor, told me about Tsui-Goab."

All around the people burst out laughing and though Garib did not know what he had said that was funny he wished the earth beneath his feet might open up and swallow him.

"Not Tsui-Goab," said Kaptein Pieter with a grin. "This God is the White Man's God."

Garib had never heard of the White Man's God. Neither had he heard of a book. He did not know what such a thing might be and in the pain of his increasing humiliation he would rather have died than have asked.

"How can a piece of rubbish know about the White Man's God?" said Hendrick. He never lost the chance to sneer at the two who had so recently been slaves. It was because of them, he said, that he had brought home so few iron beads as his prize. He especially seemed to hate Garib, as if the boy's refusal to bow his head before his taunting made him all the more determined to break him. "*Ai!*" he said. "Do not waste words on him, my Kaptein."

And after that it was not only Hendrick who sneered at them. Many of the other men and women who had at first ignored them found entertainment in shouting insults at Garib and Fast Foot as they went by.

"Do not pay heed to them, Young One," whispered Fast Foot, seeing the anger gathering in Garib's eye. "They are only jealous of your success with the cattle." He put a restraining hand on Garib's arm. "We cannot fight them for they are too many and I have heard that Haramub frowns on men

82

who fight in his village."

But as the gibes continued Garib thought that he no longer cared that the people of Niais were many and powerful and superior to all others. Rich and clever the Warlike People might be, but Garib could understand now why the old people had called them "wearers of hats" with scorn and had said that the men from the south were nothing but robbers for they were low men who did not know how to behave.

Then one afternoon as he and Fast Foot were coming back to the hut which they shared with other Nama adventurers, they had to pass Hendrick as he stood beside the path talking to some women. When he saw Garib his lip curled as always and, as if wishing to impress the women, he spat out a jet of spittle at the boy's feet. "Bushman!" he hissed.

Garib stopped in his tracks. He could bear no more of such contempt. Slowly and deliberately he stooped and picked up a handful of dust and held it out to his tormentor as he had seen other men do when they challenged another to fight.

"Garib!" cried Fast Foot, but Garib paid no heed.

"I am equal to any man of the Warlike People," he said loudly.

Hendrick stared at the dust and the people around gasped.

"Do not be fools," said someone. "The Great Chief does not allow fighting in his village."

But already a crowd was gathering. "*Ai!* Hendrick! *Ai!*" came shouts from all sides for Hendrick was not liked and many of the men were grinning with anticipation.

For a long moment Hendrick did not move, then his hand went quickly and furtively towards his gun that was slung over his shoulder. But before he could grasp it one of the men from the crowd had stepped forward. "You know the rules," he said roughly. "Either strike the young one's hand to show you accept his challenge and fight fairly as a man, or you must stand while he throws the dust into your face so that all may know you for a coward."

Garib glanced up at the man, but his anger was so great that it did not even amaze him that one of the Warlike People should speak out to protect him from Hendrick's slyness.

Hendrick scowled, but with so many eyes upon him he could

do nothing but accept the challenge. In silent fury he struck Garib's hand a vicious blow so that the sand flew up into the air. Then, tossing his gun to the ground and kicking off his sandals, he leapt at Garib and caught him by the leather cord about his neck.

"Ja ... aa!" he screamed, scratching at Garib's eyes like a wild cat.

In a moment Garib and Hendrick were rolling on the ground, striking open-handed at each other, biting, twisting, kicking, while the crowd roared with excitement at each blow.

Then Hendrick's hands were about Garib's throat and pressing inward. Gasping and choking, Garib felt himself sinking into blackness. With a tremendous effort he brought up his legs and wedged his feet against Hendrick's stomach, then with the strength of desperation, he kicked out.

With a scream of pain, Hendrick loosened his grip on Garib's throat and fell backwards. A great shout rose from the onlookers.

Garib tasted blood trickling from his lip into his mouth. The world was still swimming before his eyes. He struggled to his feet and stood swaying, his chest heaving with exertion as he waited for Hendrick to rise also.

"Come on, Hendrick!" the men shouted. "Do not lie in the dust sleeping while the young one waits!"

The words seemed to sting Hendrick back to life. He twisted into a crouching position, his face dark with hate. He stretched out and his hand closed on a large jagged piece of quartz that lay near his feet.

"Eisey!" shouted someone. "Now we will see some fighting!" But in an instant Fast Foot had pushed his way through the throng. "Stop him!" he was shouting. "He will murder the boy!"

The crowd yelled and screamed with excitement. Then with appalling suddenness there was silence. It was so unexpected that even the combatants became aware of it. Hendrick stood up, and Garib, still blinking through a haze of blood, turned to look in the direction all eyes were looking.

The crowd had parted and Haramub was standing not three paces from Garib. His stern eye took in the boy's dishevelled appearance and bleeding face, then his gaze moved to Hendrick and lingered thoughtfully on the stone in his hand.

"You fight with the man of Arub, Hendrick?" he asked grimly.

"Yes, my chief." Hendrick moved uneasily, shifting his feet in the sand, then in a sullen tone, blurted out, "This piece of rubbish said he was the equal of any man of the Warlike People!"

Haramub nodded. His shrewd eyes seemed to know exactly what had happened without being told, but he showed no relenting.

"I do not allow such a disturbance in my village for any reason as you very well know," he said in the same tone. "If you wish to fight to satisfy pride, then let your opponent be a worthy one." Haramub paused and the fearful watching crowd did not stir. "A lion is a noble beast. He is a creature men do not try to destroy unless he harms them, and then he may only be killed by real men, not by servants." He turned to Hendrick and Garib, his eyes flint-hard with purpose. "My herdsmen tell me that a lion has been worrying my cattle for the last two nights and has killed one of my oxen. Tomorrow you two men shall track this lion down and kill him as a punishment for using my home as if it were no better than the house of a wild man."

When he had gone the crowd began to disperse quickly as if they feared some awful fate might await them too if they remained. Fast Foot hurried to Garib's side.

"Young One!" he cried. "What have you done?"

"*Ai!*" said the man who had warned them against fighting, as he moved away. "If you live to see the sun set after today I think you will not be in a hurry to quarrel again when the Great Chief is near."

Nine

Garib had heard the roaring of lions many times since he had come to Niais, but in the safety of the village he had taken little notice. That night the fearful sound began soon after the people had built their cooking fires, and continued all through the long time of darkness. It sounded not unlike the trumpeting of the great bull elephants he had heard in his childhood. Garib lay wrapped in his kaross in the blackness of the hut, listening, and he knew that Fast Foot was unable to sleep either for every now and then he would whisper some fresh thought into Garib's ear.

"Do not lose courage, Young One," he said. "It is not in the nature of a lion to attack men for it is true what Haramub says. The lion is a noble beast, a brave hunter and one to be respected. It is only poverty and despair which causes these beasts to prey on the villages of men. All the game has been killed off by Haramub's guns and they are driven by hunger to become scavengers."

Later he whispered, "More men are killed by the buffalo and the leopard, Garib, than by lions. A man who is as quick and agile as you are will stand a chance even against such an opponent."

And later still, when all the other men in the hut were asleep, he said, "Only remember all that I have taught you of hunting. And do not forget to save the thrust of your knife till you find his throat for once wounded a lion will tear and rip in a madness of fury. When you stab, you must kill with your first blow or all is lost."

Slowly, and with as much careful method as he had ever shown in the preparation of his arrows and hunting poisons,

86

Fast Foot kept seeking for fresh advice which might be of help or comfort to Garib, and Garib, though he found neither help nor comfort in any of Fast Foot's words felt a vague gratitude towards the anxious man for his concern.

Turning his head, he whispered back, "Do not be worried, Fast Foot, for I am not afraid."

And indeed this seemed almost to be true. He thought fleetingly of his cowardice at the time of the battle with Kamoja, but he knew that Fast Foot had been right. He had been too young then for such a sight. Now he was older and he knew that, no matter what happened, he would not be turned to stone again by terror, and after a while he was so numbed by weariness that he fell asleep.

In the morning at the first light of dawn Haramub's servant came to fetch Garib. Garib dressed quickly in his loin skins, sandals and kaross. He picked up his long hunting knife and tied it in its sheath to his waist. Then without a glance at Fast Foot or any of the other men, he followed the servant out through the low hut door.

Quickly they went along the road between the huts to one of the folds where the calves and some other cattle were kept at night. A number of men were gathered there already. Garib saw Hendrick standing among them, his gun slung over his shoulder. For once when he saw Garib he shouted no insult. He only stared at the boy blankly with eyes that looked small and reddened and Garib knew that he had been seeking an escape from fear in the hemp pipe.

"The lion made another kill last night," said Kaptein Pieter, coming up to him. He pointed to a dead ox by the fold gate.

Silently Garib looked at it. It was a terrible sight. There were marks from the lion's teeth on the beast's throat and the skin and flesh had been torn from its hind quarters and its stomach ripped open. Garib glanced away, but not from horror, for he was still aware of the almost uncaring feeling of calm he had known in the night. He looked to see if Haramub were there to watch the two men endure their ordeal, but there was no sign of the little chief.

"We shall go on foot," said the Kaptein, "for the lion cannot

87

be far distant. He will be sleeping in some hidden place after his feast."

The lion's tracks were clear in the soft sand, broad and heavy and leading in an unbroken path towards the trees and thick bush behind the village. Pieter and Hendrick went ahead with Garib close behind and several of the other men followed. Garib saw that Fast Foot was there too, coming quickly after them with some of the village dogs, which, scenting a hunt, were running along happily, and behind all came a number of Mountain People servants, keeping at a safe distance, but eager also for the meat.

They walked for some time, following the tracks between the thickets of thorn scrub, then suddenly Pieter stopped and pointed. About two hundred paces distant, by the side of a giraffe-thorn tree, was a dusky indistinct shape.

There was silence for what seemed an endless season, then with a low angry growl the lion rose to his feet. He had a great head and long black mane, and at the sound of the menacing rumble that rose in his throat the dogs which had been running ahead, came slinking back towards the men with their tails between their legs and the hair on the backs of their necks standing upright like the bristles of a warthog.

The lion turned his head and looked at the men, then suddenly bounded two paces towards them. It was a movement so rapid, so silent and smooth, that for a moment the people were paralysed with shock. Then with screams of *"Gnoo! Gnoo!* Sit! Sit!"* they leapt into the bushes on both sides for it was well known among them that it was useless to run from a lion and that the beast was less likely to attack a person sitting or lying than one standing in his path. Kaptein Pieter and Hendrick and Garib were left alone.

Slowly and smoothly the lion began to walk towards them. Kaptein Pieter stepped back hurriedly and, shivering with fright, Hendrick fell on to one knee and raised his gun to his shoulder. Garib could hear his teeth chattering.

"Make ready, Garib, the lion is coming!" called out Fast Foot.

Garib threw off his kaross and kicked off his sandals as Fast Foot had taught him to do when hunting so long ago.

He drew his knife from its sheath and moved silently as a shadow to a nearby bush.

As the lion advanced he looked as harmless as a big yellow dog, his head far too large for his thin mangy body. Indeed he did not look a noble creature as a lion should. Then, at a distance of about a hundred paces he stopped again, sniffing at the air, and in a moment his whole appearance changed. His great mouth opened in a tearing, hissing snarl, displaying all his teeth, and his dark mane came erect, every hair of it standing on end so that the beast seemed to swell as if by some magic to the size of an ox.

"*Eisey!*" screamed Hendrick, gripping his gun in terror.

"Do not shoot, you fool!" shouted Kaptein Pieter. "You are too far away. You will only wound him!"

It was too late. There was a flash of flame and a shattering explosion and the lion wheeled about, then fell to the ground and rolled over in the dust.

"I hit him! I hit him!" shouted Hendrick, but the next instant the lion was on his feet again and with an ear-splitting roar of rage and pain came dashing through the bushes towards them. Leaping into the air over a rock, he tore a portion from it with his hind claws and came to earth, growling, his great head between his forepaws and his long tufted tail lashing at the ground in fury as he prepared to spring.

The next moment the lion was upon Garib. He was thrown to the ground under the beast's great weight, his knife pinned under him. The lion twisted his head in a terrible snarl. Garib could feel his hot fetid breath full upon his face; see the yellow eyes, mad with fury, so close to his own. Then the lion brought a heavy paw down upon Garib's arm. Garib could feel no pain, only a warmth which he knew to be his own blood.

He remembered the sight of the ox outside the cattle enclosure. Soon he too would be nothing but a torn and ripped hunk of meat. There was to be no glory, only this. And suddenly he hated the great body that lay upon him with a hatred so fierce that it was like a fire consuming him. All his disillusionment and disappointment, all his loathing of the vile slavery to which he had been subjected by Kamoja and his

89

bitter resentment of the contempt which he had suffered at the hands of Haramub's people, seemed to well up in him so that, though he gave no thought to any of these things, they became part of the wound in his arm and, like the lion, he too was crazed with fear and fury.

The madness gave him a strength which he had never before possessed. He writhed and twisted under the snarling, clutching beast until his arm was freed from under him. Gripping his knife, he found the beast's throat and plunged it into the fur with all his might.

The lion roared and rolled over. With a heave he reared away from Garib and in a mounting frenzy of pain, with Garib's knife still embedded in his throat, staggered to and fro, crashing into bushes and breaking down branches till the sand all around was one great patch of blood. Then with a shuddering sigh he sank to the ground and lay still.

Panting and gasping, Garib watched him, then, when he saw that the lion was dead, he too rolled over and closed his eyes. He heard shouting and the sound of running feet, but the noise seemed to come from a great distance. He was aware only of a terrible desolation as if he was the only man left alive upon a vast arid plain that stretched to the end of the world. And with the desolation came the beginning of pain. It was as if every piece of his flesh had been torn from his bones by the savage beast. He did not know that Fast Foot was bending over him, weeping and blabbering like a woman, or that the Mountain People were already busy with their knives, skinning the dead lion. He did not even know when he was lifted by Fast Foot and the Kaptein and carried back to the village. He knew only that he wished to die more than anything in the world.

For three days and three nights Garib lay between life and death. Many times he wished to slip away into that strange grey place of peace which seemed so near but each time a voice called him back though Garib had no idea where he was or who was calling.

"Garib! Garib!" the voice kept saying. "You are too young to die. Do not lose courage, Young One. I am with you."

Then on the third day he opened his eyes. The pain in his body was still there, gnawing like a rat at his limbs, but it no longer consumed him. He gazed up weakly and saw that he was in his own hut, lying on his own kaross in the hollow he had dug for himself in the hard earth floor. As he sighed a man got up and bent over him and then Garib knew who had spoken to him so often in his delirium.

"*Ai*, Young One!" whispered Fast Foot as if he dared not even speak in a normal tone lest he send Garib back to the world of death from which he had just come. He held a cup to Garib's lips and with a gentleness Garib had not even known from his own mother, slid a hand under his head to lift it so that he could drink.

"Fast Foot?"

"You will be well now, Young One," the hunter said soothingly as if he were speaking to a child. "Your wounds were deep and the claws and teeth of a wild beast contain much poison. No, do not try to move for Haramub's doctor of herbs has placed poultices upon your torn arm and the great gash in your thigh."

"Haramub?"

"Yes, Young One. Every day Haramub the chief has sent his doctor and bowls of food which you could not eat."

Garib tried to understand, but he was still too weak and already he was drifting back into a haze of pain and confusion.

"Sleep, Young One," said Fast Foot. "Sleep."

Day followed day and slowly Garib grew stronger. His periods of clarity increased and he needed to sleep less and less. At first the doctor, a small cheerful man with many horns and boxes of ointments and medicines hanging from his neck, called every day, then his visits too became less frequent, and after a while Fast Foot too was able to leave him and return to his work at the cattle pen, for, as he told Garib, Haramub was planning to move his village, though no one knew to which place, and there were many ride and pack oxen to be broken into service for the journey.

Then one day while Garib was lying alone in the hut there was a small commotion at the entrance and someone entered through the door. Garib could not turn his head to look for

91

the wound in his arm was still too stiff. The man came quickly towards him and squatted down beside him. It was Haramub himself.

"Greetings, Garib Arub," he said, and to Garib's astonishment he smiled. It was a modest, friendly smile, such as one man might give to another. In surprise and confusion Garib could only stare at the man who so recently had condemned him to a struggle for his very life with a great and savage beast.

"Greetings, my chief," he said.

"So, Garib," Haramub went on in the same unassuming and friendly way. "My doctor tells me that you will soon be well. That is good news. I have been speaking also to the master of my oxen and he tells me that you have a way with beasts and can train them without the use of fire to do your bidding. This too is good news, Garib Arub, for a man shows his lack of command when he must use brute force to make others obey."

"*A*, my chief," murmured Garib, hardly knowing if he might believe this unexpected praise.

"The Kaptein Pieter speaks well of you too, Garib," said Haramub. "He says you fought against the bad lion with the fierceness of three men. He did not know that so slender a boy could possess such a will to live!"

Haramub's smile broadened and he gave a pleasant laugh. "*Ai*, Garib! All in all I am pleased with you for I remember you from that time many seasons ago when I visited the village of Arub the Big One and you ran after my horse. Yes, Garib," he said. "This surprises you, does it not for you thought I had forgotten? But when you know me better you will know that not only do I insist on absolute obedience to all my laws—" He did not stop smiling but he paused slightly and the meaning of his words was not lost on the one who still carried the wounds of Haramub's punishment "—but I also forget nothing. That is why men should walk with care when in my presence."

Garib gazed up at Haramub in blank astonishment. So the little chief *had* recognized him that first day!

"So, Garib Arub, I have been watching you for though I knew you to have been a boy of spirit I knew also that you had since been a slave, and some men, once they have known bondage, remain slaves forever. But I saw that you still held your head with pride and kicked against the insults of my people and I thought that, though you had sunk so low as to be a Black Man's slave, you might still be of use to me."

To be of use to him. These were the same words the little chief had used so long ago when he had spoken of his great dream of conquering the whole land of the Cattle People and making it his home. Indeed, thought Garib with a wildly beating heart, Haramub had not forgotten his promise!

"So I thought to find a test wherein you might prove yourself to me, man of Arub," said Haramub mildly.

A test! Garib stared at Haramub in shock as the meaning of these words too reached him. A chill hand seemed to close about him when he thought of how cold and calculating this test had been. To prove Garib's usefulness to him in his vision of glory he had been willing to risk the boy's life without the slightest qualm, and Garib knew then, as he looked into the eyes which were smiling upon him with such friendliness, that if he had been killed Haramub would have shed no tears nor felt any remorse, for Garib's defeat would have proved that he was not made of the metal Haramub needed in men to achieve his goal and was therefore of no moment whatsoever. Never before had he met in a man such deadly singleness of purpose.

"Now you have proved yourself to be, though little more than a boy, a man of courage and resource," Haramub was saying. "And so I tell you, you must make haste to become strong again for I need you now to help prepare my oxen, for, as you may have heard, I intend to move my village. This place is no longer good enough for me. The veld is grazed off by all my cattle and the game has disappeared."

Garib felt a quick pang of disappointment. Was this then the work Haramub had had in mind for him? That he be nothing more than another herdsman in his town?

"A, khub," he said quickly to hide his feelings. "To what place are we going?"

The smile faded on Haramub's face and Garib saw that the chief did not like to be asked more than he had thought fitting to tell. He stood up.

"That you will see soon enough, Garib Arub," he said with a hint of coldness. He turned to go, then paused. He looked down thoughtfully at Garib a moment longer, then smiling again suddenly said, "But this much I shall tell you for I think you are a man who knows enough to keep his voice silent. The Cattle People are uncountable in number and they are like the lions who attack fiercely and in the night. At the place to which I plan to go I may have use for men who are capable of killing lions."

Lying alone Garib thought of what Haramub had said and he was coldly aware that if another occasion arose when the little chief, for some purpose of his own, felt it necessary to risk Garib's life, he would do so without a qualm. He knew this, yet he knew with even greater certainty that he too wished to follow Haramub. With a growing feeling of wonder, it seemed to Garib that suddenly the mists of confusion and despair had been lifted from his eyes and, stretching out before him in such clarity that he could scarcely lie still for his eagerness and excitement, was a shining road leading straight to glory.

Ten

In his eagerness to be ready for whatever work it was that Haramub might have in store for him, Garib recovered quickly. His wounds healed until they were nothing but purple scars on his arm and thigh and he was able to return to his tasks among the oxen.

But now he was no longer content to be merely one of the many young men dragging on the thongs which held the bucking beasts while the master of the oxen tied the packs upon their untrained backs. Now, in his longing to prove yet again to Haramub his worthiness, he asked permission to be one of the riders who broke in the new oxen as ride-oxen. This was the most dangerous work and only the most skilled were willing or able to tackle it.

The master of the oxen laughed. "Kill yourself if you wish," he said and shouted to the men to secure one of the roaring, terrified beasts and bring it out of the fold.

When the stick had been thrust through the ox's nose and the thong fastened to it as a bridle, sheep skins were placed on its back and secured with more thongs round the body. The men held the snorting beast down by the bridle and the tail while Garib mounted, then with shouts and cries, they let go and rushed in all directions to safety.

At the beast's first furious plunge, Garib was hurled to the ground. He was on his feet again in a moment and leaping out of the enraged creature's path. The men watching roared with laughter.

"Have you had enough?" asked the master, grinning, when Garib reached the stone wall of the stockade.

Garib hated the laughter but he forced down his anger.

"Let the men catch the ox again," he said. "I will do better this time."

Time after time Garib was thrown from the plunging, bellowing ox, but he would not give up and after a while he learnt, by gripping fast to the belly thongs and digging his knees into the beast's sides, to keep his seat. The ox kicked and galloped and bucked. It rushed through bushes and under low trees in an effort to rid itself of its unaccustomed burden, but all in vain. Scratched and battered and bruised, Garib hung on and at last, exhausted, the ox tossed its long horns and came to a standstill.

The next day Garib fought the same ox again, and the next, and by the end of the fourth day the ox accepted its rider without protest. It was broken in.

That night a servant arrived at Garib's hut with an armful of clothes. He handed the astonished Garib a pair of leather trousers and a shirt and a wide-brimmed hat.

"The chief sends greetings," said the servant. "I carry also his words, master. He says, 'One who can act like a man must dress like a man and not a Bushman.'"

Garib had never before been called "master" by any man in Niais, not even a servant. He took the clothes and felt the cloth of the shirt with pleasure, then put them on hastily and turned to Fast Foot.

"*Ai!*" exclaimed the hunter in amazement. "*Ai*, Garib! You look just like one of the men from the south!" There was an expression almost of awe on his face and he spoke with unaccustomed restraint.

Garib laughed. "Fast Foot, do not gaze at me so strangely. I am still Garib Arub even though I wear these fine clothes." But even as he spoke he knew that this was not the complete truth. Looking down at the new trousers, he thought that people could no longer sneer at him as being nothing but an ignorant man of the Nama nation. Already he had the look of one of the men of Haramub so that even Fast Foot had spoken as to a superior stranger. And Garib resolved to learn all he could of the ways the Warlike People had learnt from the White Men in the south. He could not imagine what a White Man might look like, but he knew from what he had already seen, that it was these ways and weapons which were giving Haramub and his men their power.

After that Garib worked even harder to become a good cattle man and as he began to earn cattle and sheep for his work he bartered some of them for a metal bucket and a black pot from Kaptein Pieter. And whenever he had the chance he listened carefully to the strange language Haramub and his men had learnt from their Dutch masters, and he began to dream of the day when he, Garib, would own a horse and a gun also.

He tried to persuade Fast Foot to acquire White Men's clothing and possessions too, but the hunter only threw up his hands in alarm.

"No, no, Young One," he said. "I am too old for such strange magic. I would not feel at ease with hard leather keeping my legs from freedom."

Garib was vaguely disappointed, but he saw that Fast Foot was not one who yearned for new experiences, and as the moons passed he found himself more and more in the company of the younger men of Niais and saw less of his older friend.

Then towards the end of the summer Haramub called the people together and told them that he and the Elders of the village had decided it was now time to move the huts to a place of better pasturage.

"Many seasons ago," said Haramub, "when travelling through the country I came upon a valley among the mountains which was the most beautiful and fertile place I had ever seen and I thought, 'This is a fitting home for the one Haramub who is also called Jonker Afrikaner.' In the centre of this valley, among rocks of granite, rose up a warm spring, the water of which flowed freely and plentifully down on to the plain below. To mark the spot I built a dam across the stream and planted the seeds of a calabash there as a promise to myself that one day I would return with my tribe to eat its fruits."

The people listened eagerly, anxious to hear at last where this land was.

"But," went on Haramub, "I had to delay going there for this place I speak of is on the very border of the land of the

97

Cattle People. I had to wait first for my tribe to grow in strength so that we could safeguard our people and our cattle from attack. But now," he said, looking round calmly, "I shall delay no longer. We leave at the full of the moon!"

The people could speak of nothing else but the astonishing news and Garib saw with some surprise that the Warlike People, for all their boasting, were not a brave people. They were filled with fear at the thought of moving so close to the hated Black Men.

But he saw too that they shared his confidence in the strength of their chief. "Haramub is with us. He knows how to deal with the Cattle People," they said again and again. And when at last they set out with their huts and possessions packed on to the pack oxen, and the women and children upon their ride oxen, and the men on their fine horses, and the rest of the people and servants coming along behind in a long procession with the cattle, there was not one who stayed behind.

They journeyed through lovely country abounding in trees, and after two days they approached the land where Haramub had built his dam. They came through a pass in the jagged rocky hills where orange stones and pebbles lay upon the pale soil and hundreds of grass nests of the weaver birds hung, safe from baboons and snakes, at the ends of the branches, and the valley opened up before them.

It was a wide plain, stretching east and west, enclosed by mountains on three sides, and upon it lay a forest of thorn trees, and the grass, yellow with the season, stood tall and strong, and because no hunters dwelt there with their guns, there was an abundance of game. Pheasants and guinea fowl ran about among the shrubs and deer stood half-hidden in the thickets and from all sides came the song of birds.

And while the people were cooking meat and refreshing themselves before undertaking the last of the journey which would bring them to the hot springs, Garib turned from gazing at the view and found Haramub standing beside him. He was not wearing the hard expression of Haramub the Great One, but that other informal, friendly look he had worn when he had been in Garib's hut and away from the eyes of his people.

"Do you see those mountains?" he asked, pointing. "They

remind me of the mountains around the place to the south of the Great River where I was born. The Winterhoek they were called. It is a word in the language of the Dutch White Men and it means the Winter Corner because in times of frost the people in the neighbourhood could find protected places in the big kloof between the hills where their herds could graze in ease. It was a place of shelter and safety and I shall call this valley Winterhoek* also for it shall give my homeless people a place of shelter and safety where they may live."

"A, khub," said Garib, and touched by Haramub's soft tone he thought a little wistfully of the country of his own birth among the Hills of the Killing of the Elephant. "It is a good valley for a home."

The little chief turned to Garib quickly. Usually he kept his own counsel and spoke no more than was necessary as if he felt strength lay in silence, but today, perhaps because even one as great as Haramub might become excited when he saw a dream about to become reality, or perhaps because he saw the sympathy in the boy's eyes, he became talkative.

"Yes, Garib Arub," he said. "My people have wandered far and have known great suffering because they had no home. They were driven from their pastures by the White Men and forced further and further north, but there was no land they might call their own. Everywhere the White Men followed. They shot off all the game with their guns and stole the water-holes, and at last, so that our tribe might not all die of hunger, my father and his people had to become the servants of one of the new Dutch farmers, a big White Man named Piet Pienaar."

At the mention of this strange name anger kindled suddenly in Haramub's face. "Ai!" he cried. "This was a cruel man. Did I not see with my own eyes when still a child how he beat his servants with a sjambok.† I do not know why he hated our people for my father was a good shepherd to him, but he kicked us and beat us and treated us worse than dogs!"

Garib had never seen Haramub angry before, but with each

---

* Later the place where Jonker Afrikaner built his town became known as Windhoek and is today the capital of South-West-Africa.
† A leather baton used like a club for punishment.

word he spoke about this cruel White Man the flame of his wrath seemed to grow until it was a great fire of hatred.

"So it was, Garib," he said. "The master Pienaar said that all we were good for was to hunt the little Bushmen who hid in the hills and stole his cattle when there was no game left to eat. He gave my father and his men guns and powder and taught them how to kill for him. He taught them how to attack at night and shoot the people and carry off any goods they could find in payment for the stolen beasts.

"Then one day my father refused to do any more killing because Pienaar did not act justly towards the people. The master was very angry. When my father went to the house to answer his shouts, Pienaar rushed out with his gun and knocked my father down and in the fight that followed someone took the gun and shot Piet Pienaar. And when the people saw that he was dead they were afraid of the anger of the other White Men and so they took all the weapons and ammunition they could find and fled to the vast lands along the Great River."

Garib could understand Haramub's anger. He knew how easily hurt were the little Men of Men and how sensitive they were to any slight or insult to their dignity. And he knew how suffering might turn to hatred and hatred to a determination for revenge, even as he himself was one day determined to kill Kahitjene, the unknown Cattle King, so that hurt might pay for hurt and the debt be settled. But Piet Pienaar was dead. Were not the wrongs of Haramub's people already avenged? Garib could not understand why after so long a season of time the little chief continued to hate with such fierceness, and, knowing that he was hearing what few other men had ever heard from Haramub's lips, he listened in awe.

"But though we were without a home," went on Haramub with frightening intensity, "we were not helpless for we had the guns and Piet Pienaar had taught us how to rob and plunder. It was not long before my father's name was whispered in terror throughout the length and breadth of the land. *Ai*, yes! We had learnt much cleverness from our master. My father said to us that we would prove to the people that we were men of importance and not, as the master had said, brown rubbish. Do you know, Garib, that Piet Pienaar would not even read to us out of the Book of the White Men which told about God? When the people came to his house to ask to hear the Word, the master said that we were not fit to be told of God for we were lower than baboons and worse than dogs."

Haramub stopped. A childlike look of hurt and confusion passed quickly over his face and in a flash Garib remembered his own hurt and fury at Hendrick's insults. Haramub's praise and acceptance of him had healed the wound so that he no longer felt hatred, but he saw now, with disconcerting clarity, that Haramub's wound had been too deep and had not been healed by acceptance. And suddenly he thought he understood the cold ruthlessness he had sometimes felt in the little chief. He knew from his own fight with the lion of how a wild beast, when wounded, would turn with a fury beyond even the fierceness of its own nature upon its attacker, and he had often heard men say that if such a beast lived on and the wound did not heal, in its festering pain, the lion would afterwards tear to pieces all who came near as if it wished to avenge itself not only on the one who had caused the hurt, but on the whole world.

As quickly as it had come, the look of bewilderment was gone. For a moment it had been as if Haramub the child had stood before Garib; now Haramub the man, as if angry that even for one unguarded moment he had allowed such weakness to show, strove to cover his embarrassment.

He turned back to Garib, and now it was not excitement which caused him to be more talkative than was his custom but the hurry to hide confusion. "My father could have been a great man," he cried, "but by then he was old and, like an old lion, he wished for nothing more than to lie in the sun. Then the White missionaries, the Men of God, arrived one day at his village, and because he wished to prove to all that his people were indeed fit to hear the Word of God, he allowed them to come and teach him their wisdom. And then he had to give up raiding for the God of the White Men demands peace, and the missionary Moffat took my father and me also on a long journey to the furthest south to receive pardon for our crimes from the White Men's chief in a place named Cape Town. *Ai, Garib!*" he said, and suddenly his eyes were shining, "that was a great town. I tell you, no man of the Men of Men could even dream of such greatness."

He paused as if to collect his thoughts which had been scattered by the memory of such glory, then he said abruptly, "Soon after we returned my father died and then our people divided. Some wished to stay with the Men of God, but the rest came with me and became known as the Warlike People. The missionaries are of use only to old men. We were young and we wished for more than wisdom with which to fill our cattle folds. And that was when I met you, Garib, when I was still a homeless wanderer—"

He stopped again and Garib wondered if, unbidden, his thoughts had once more turned to suffering, for he frowned. "But what does it profit a man to dwell on what is past," he said loudly. "What is past is dead." He kicked angrily at a stone as if to convince both it and himself that this was true. "It is the present which must give us joy, and, as you see, the present is good!" he cried. "At last I have brought my people to this promised valley and never again shall I be the servant of others. From this high place I shall make myself master of the whole land. From these mountains I can bring all the tribes of the Nama nation under my control and I am also close to the great wealth of the Cattle People."

Haramub looked quickly at Garib. "Yes, we are closer here to the Cattle People than you guess," he said. "Just over those mountains are the great herds of Kahitjene." The little chief smiled with satisfaction as he saw the astonishment on Garib's face. "Yes, Young One," he said. "I remember that this is the man you have sworn to kill. You wish for his blood and I wish for his cattle. But I warn you, Garib Arub, do not hunt this jackal unless I give the word. You are now one of my people and I have many plans for my tribe. In this new valley of the Winterhoek we shall grow in strength until we are truly greater than all others."

Eleven

When at last the great procession of people and beasts reached Haramub's dam, they saw it was indeed a good place for a home. They found themselves in a wooded valley where everything was gold, green and brown in the winter sunshine. The hot springs the chief had told them about rushed out from limestone rock near the base of a high tree-covered hill and the people were so astonished at the steam which rose in clouds from the earth that they at once called the place, *Ai-gams*, The Hot Water. The water poured out in a clear stream that was caught in Haramub's dam, then, running over, it was lost in the grass and thorn trees of the valley.

And not only was the new place beautiful, it could also provide the people with all they required. There was water in inexhaustible supply, and if more were needed in time of drought it could be dug for in the bed of a wide river, dry now with the season, which wound between the mountains below the springs. There was also sufficient grazing nearby for the milch cows of a large village and pasturage in abundance for Haramub's herds of cattle in the next valley. There was plenty of wood for cooking fires and so much game that in those early days it was not necessary to slaughter any sheep or oxen for the pot.

Soon a town had sprung up between the trees on the hill above the springs, the reed-roofed huts of the Men of Men side by side with the pointed huts of branches and grass of their many servants. And after the rains in the spring the new home seemed even more beautiful, for then the water stood in pools in the valley and everything was green.

"Now my people have no need to wander further," said

Haramub. "They shall not be driven by hunger or thirst like Bushmen to keep moving their homes." And Garib saw that he did not sit back and dream with the hemp pipe as Arub the Big One had done upon arriving at his new home. With energy which astonished Garib even more than the steam had done, he set about fulfilling his promise to make his people superior to all others.

He made the servants dig a huge garden below the springs. Garib had never before heard of a man planting seeds or reaping harvest, for the people of the Nama nation did not know of such things. They knew only how to kill game and dig for roots and bulbs for food. Now he watched carefully, eager to learn everything new so that he could truly become one of Haramub's people.

Then Haramub set about building a great house, the like of which Garib had also never dreamed of, out of stone dug from the hillside. It was longer and wider than six huts and more than twice as tall, and it had a door through which a man could walk without stooping, and holes high up in the walls, through which the light could enter. Kaptein Pieter told Garib that it was like the houses the White Men built in the south, and when it was finished the women hardened the earth floor with mud and the men made long strange seats of wood and the servants crushed lime and made it into paint and rubbed it on to the walls with their hands until the whole building shone with whiteness in the sun.

Garib thought there could surely be no more wonders which Haramub knew of, but in this he was mistaken, for as soon as the first rains were over the little chief started work again, this time on a road—not a path beaten by the hooves of cattle or elephants such as Garib knew, but a great wide road made by the hands of men. The people had to remove stones and dig out rocks and uproot trees and bushes until a wide straight track was made that led right over the mountains.

But by now Garib was no longer shy to ask questions for the people of Ai-gams seemed to accept him as one of themselves. Even Hendrick, though he sometimes scowled sullenly, no longer insulted him, and indeed it was Hendrick who told Garib the reason for the road.

"The Great Chief wishes the White Men to come to his town and so he clears a way for them," he said.

"The White Men!" exclaimed Garib.

"*A*," said Hendrick as if it gave him pleasure that he still knew more than Garib. "Haramub needs more guns and more ammunition and powder for the guns. Where shall he get them except from the White Men, and it is too far to travel to the south every time he needs fresh supplies. The White Men have a place to the west by the sea where the ships call to get water and meat from the tribes."

"*Eisey!*" said Garib, but by now he had learnt so much from listening and asking questions that he knew that there were such things as ships and wagons and wheels, and he had even heard of the harbour of which Hendrick spoke on the coast a long distance away. And soon, it seemed, he would know what a White Man looked like also. He remembered all that he had heard of this powerful people who lived across the Great River and, who, though their God demanded peace, taught men to kill, and he watched the road lengthening out with great apprehension.

During all this time Haramub spoke but little to Garib. When not occupied in sitting with his Council of Elders, the chief was busy visiting his road or inspecting his stone building. He was everywhere at once, walking swiftly, always stern and thoughtful, watching over his town with the eye of a hawk. If he found men fighting, he had them beaten. If he heard them becoming disorderly over the pots of honey beer he went himself and emptied the brew on to the ground. And Garib, seeing that the splendour of Ai-gams was fast surpassing even that of Niais, waited impatiently for Haramub to call him so that he might share in the glory.

Then one day while Garib and Fast Foot were working in the cattle enclosure they heard a great shout. "They are coming! The White Men are coming!" At once the paths between the huts were filled with excited people.

Garib and Fast Foot hurried after them. They stopped on the rocks above the hot springs and stared down Haramub's road that cut a path through the thorn trees of the valley to the mountains. In the distance was a cloud of pale dust and coming out of it was what looked like a great grey-white beast with other dark shapes following behind.

"Wagons!" said Garib, and in spite of his own uneasiness he almost laughed as he turned and saw Fast Foot's astonished awe-stricken face.

"*Eisey!*" whispered the hunter. He had still not troubled to learn much of Haramub's language and he was even less prepared for the frightening sight than Garib. "How many oxen does it take to pull these fierce monsters?"

As the first wagon came nearer they saw that a man of the Nama nation was leading the oxen and another was sitting upon a box in the front holding a long whip. The wagon wheels were sinking deeply into the loose soil, lifting large quantities of sand on the spokes which fell again like water from a waterfall as they turned, and though the wheels themselves made little sound, all else was noise and confusion. The great cart thumped and creaked as the oxen strained to pull its heavy weight, the whip cracked like rifle shots in the dry air, the leader shouted and yelled, and every now and then the driver leapt from his seat to urge the oxen on to greater effort with flailing whip and screams of abuse.

And as the wagon train approached the town the confusion became even greater for then several of the men ran out to help, twisting the tails of the oxen and biting them to make the stubborn beasts move on, and the village dogs joined in in a frenzy of yelping and barking.

Garib stared as the wagon with its rowdy helpers passed by and creaked and groaned its way up the rise to the huts. Walking calmly beside it were the men Garib had come to see— the White Men. He was half-disappointed, half-relieved. There was nothing terrifying in their appearance. They were dressed in ordinary clothes of dark cloth and wide-brimmed hats, and their skin was not white. It was just paler than that of the Men of Men. Even their expressions were not fearsome. Like any other men after a long journey the White Men were plodding wearily through the sand, their faces stained with dust.

Garib saw Kaptein Pieter standing near him.

"My Kaptein," he said eagerly. "Shall I be able to buy a

horse and a gun from these men?"

Kaptein Pieter looked at him in surprise. "No, Lion-Killer," he said, laughing. "These are not traders. These are the Men of God whom Haramub has called to teach his people."

The Men of God! Garib gasped in astonishment. Why had Haramub called for these men? Had the little chief gone mad, or was he, like his father, wishing only to prove that his people were also good enough to hear of the White Men's God? But the little chief himself had told Garib that the missionaries demanded peace and were of use only to old men. How then could these Men of God help the Warlike People to greatness?

Twelve

Garib sat on the hard wooden bench in the white-washed building the men of Ai-gams called the church. The place was filled with people, men, women and children, and those who had arrived too late to find a seat were crowded together at the back, and, as always whenever anything new was happening, there was much noise and excited chatter. The people had been ordered to gather here by Haramub himself to meet the missionaries and to hear the Word of God, and all around Garib those who had known the White Men in the south were telling of what they remembered of this Word which was to be found in the Book.

Garib listened in growing awe. He had not taken part in any kind of worship since leaving his home for the god of the Cattle People was not the god of the Men of Men, and Haramub's tribe paid little heed to Tsui-Goab either. At the thought of prayer Garib was aware of a thrill of uneasiness passing through him which was somehow like the echo of some ancient fear. He remembered that he had often had this same feeling when listening to the shouts of the priests in his old home, but now it was much stronger. It was as if the old fear were joined with his new fear of the ways of the White Men and he moved restlessly.

Then suddenly a man near the door shouted, "The Men of God are here!" Garib wished to run out of the strange building, away from its confining walls that seemed about to trap him, out into the sun and air and the things that he knew. But he did not move. He remained seated and gazed straight ahead.

Haramub led the way down the aisle between the benches,

and behind him came the three White Men. They walked to the end of the church and took their places in front of the people.

There was a breathless hush as Haramub mounted the steps of the stand men called the pulpit.

"Men of Ai-gams!" he said solemnly. "When I brought you to this good valley of the Winterhoek it was a joyful day. Now I tell you that this is a happy day also, for the Men of God heard of my desire that a missionary should come and teach my people and now they stand before you. When I was a boy I looked upon the great city of the White Men, Cape Town, and I saw with my own eyes the mighty power of God who had shown White Men how to accomplish such works. And remembering this I have long desired that I and my people should be taught such things also. Now I have found a place for a mission station, one with a plentiful supply of water and I wish that the Word of God may be heard not only at Ai-gams, but throughout all the land."

The people murmured in approval and some of them shouted in praise of Haramub, and Garib, in a haze of fear and confusion, listened and he realized that this coming of the Men of God was no sudden happening. Even when Haramub had stood looking at the valley of the Winterhoek with him and had spoken of greatness the little chief must have had plans to receive the missionaries, and he knew that once again he had shown his youth and ignorance when he had thought that his own dream of glory could be the same as that dreamed by one as great as Haramub. Haramub's vision was beyond anything Garib could have imagined.

The little chief held up his hand and at once there was silence. "And so, my people," he said, "I ask you to learn from these men for they have come from far. They have come from across the sea and have left many things besides their friends so that they may assist us. By them we shall be taught to know what good is."

Then Haramub stepped down and indicated to one of the White Men that he should speak. The missionary stood up and mounted the steps. He was dressed in a long dark robe and on his head was a small cap and his movements were slow

109

and deliberate. When he reached the top he turned and, placing his hands on either side of the great thick Book which lay upon the stand, he leaned forward and gazed at the people. On his chin was a dark beard and on his lip a thick moustache which filled Garib with wonder for the hair upon the faces of the Men of Men did not grow so profusely. But it was the man's eyes which impressed Garib most. Though mild in expression, their gaze was so steady that it seemed that the missionary was looking right into the hearts of the men who sat below him.

Then he spoke in the language Garib had learned from Haramub's people and his voice was as quiet and steady as his gaze. He said, "I have come to tell you of the love of God, Jehovah, the Lord of Heaven, as it is written in the Great Book so that you may be set free from your sins and may at last be brought out of darkness into God's marvellous light."

The people sat in polite silence as the missionary opened the Book and found the place with his finger. "Behold, the days come, saith the Lord God, that I will send a famine in the land, not a famine of bread, nor a thirst for water, but of hearing the words of the Lord. And they shall wander from sea to sea, and from the north even to the east, they shall run to and fro to seek the word of the Lord, and shall not find it."

The Man of God looked up and paused and Garib was aware of a feeling of shock. Suddenly for a confused moment he was back in the hut of the old soothsayer in the place of Games the queen and he was hearing the old man's whisper, "All men are seekers but their eyes are shut like the eyes of blind men and they know not where to seek or even what it is that they seek. They stumble and fall and follow many roads and still arrive at no place."

But there was no time to think for the Man of God was speaking again. "So now I have come to you so that you may cease your wandering and find God, for it is written, 'Blessed are they that hunger and thirst after righteousness for they shall be filled', and also, 'I your God, will give unto him that is athirst of the fountain of the water of life freely. He that overcometh shall inherit all things and I will be his God and he shall be my son.'"

Now some of the people began to murmur again and one who had heard the strange Word before shouted, "Praise to God!"

Then the missionary looked up and said, "And because of this love of God I have come to tell you that you have sinned. You have followed the paths of evil! I have come to tell you that it is an evil to steal the cattle of another and to make war and rob and plunder, for, even as the road of good leads to fullness of life, so the road of wickedness leads to destruction, and all those who follow it shall have their part in the lake which burneth with fire and brimstone and shall be utterly destroyed!"

There was complete silence in the church. One of the women near Garib gave a scream and fell to the floor in a faint and had to be carried out into the air, and, as if inspired by her conduct, several others began to groan and shudder, but Garib was aware only of greater and ever greater confusion. It seemed to him that he had heard all that the missionary said before. The words kept getting muddled in his head with what the soothsayer and Tomarib had told him. "Tsui-Goab is good but Gaunab is evil and if a man wishes to live he must not allow Gaunab to catch him for Gaunab is the Destroyer, and the Bringer of Death." And round and round in his head went the words, "good", "evil", "darkness", "light".

The missionary raised his hand and the commotion subsided. "But God does not desire the death of a sinner," he said sternly, "and because he does not wish men to die he sent his Son, Jesus, to bring the good news of God's love to all on earth so that whosoever keep his Word and believeth on Him shall not perish but have everlasting life."

The tumult broke out again, many of the people being now affected, crying out and praying aloud and sighing, and the weeping at the door was so loud that Garib could scarcely hear what the missionary was saying.

"Thou shalt not kill. Thou shalt not steal. Thou shalt not envy, and if there be any other commandment, it is briefly comprehended in this saying, namely, thou shalt love thy neighbour as thyself: for he that loveth another even as God

111

loves him hath fulfilled the law."

And then even the missionary had to raise his voice. "And so it must be. We must love our enemies for they are also our neighbours, and live in peace, for so it is written. 'The wolf shall dwell with the lamb and the leopard shall lie down with the kid; and the calf and the young lion and the fatling together and a little child shall lead them. They shall not hurt nor destroy in all my holy mountain for the earth shall be full of the knowledge of the Lord, as the waters cover the sea.' "

Then the Man of God bowed his head. "Amen," he said, and, closing the Book, climbed down from the pulpit.

Garib stared at him in amazement. The wolf shall dwell with the lamb! This he had never heard before from anyone and now he knew that when he had thought in that time of confinement before he was made a man that all wisdom had no meaning, he had surely been right. Had he not many times seen the lambs which the wolves* had torn to pieces in the night? How could they ever live together? How could men love their enemies? Did not all peoples hate and despise those who were not of their own kind? The Men of Men in their arrogance and pride had scorned the Mountain People who were their servants, detested the lowly Bushmen for being in appearance too much like themselves, and hated with a bitter and fearful hatred the big Cattle People who had driven them from their own country. How could it ever be otherwise when among the Men of Men themselves the different clans were so divided by jealousy that they had not been able to come together even in the time of greatest danger?

But it seemed to Garib that the people about him were even more confused than he was for, still overcome with the emotion roused up by the missionary's threat of utter destruction, several of the chief men leapt up and shouted out their feelings.

"Praise to God who has taught us to know good from evil!" cried one and the man who had spoken out for fair play during Garib's fight with Hendrick shouted, "We are like a solid block of wood, cut for making a wooden vessel, but the block

*The hyena in South-West-Africa was often called a wolf.

has no place to hold milk for our hearts are closed. There is no place for the Word of God. Now the missionaries tell us we are sinners and we know in ourselves that this is true. It is not right to kill and plunder. The Men of God at the Great River told us the same thing. Now we must listen to them. We must open our hearts. Let us show our neighbours that we have changed!"

Then Haramub jumped up again and said, "We are much moved by the words of the Men of God. We must now show them our gratitude so that they will stay with us and continue to teach us in all ways," and leading the way to a clearing outside the church, he called to his servants to bring the presents he had prepared for the White Men. One cow, five sheep and a goat were given to the missionaries, and on the ground at their feet the servants laid a kudu skin, an elephant tusk and eight sjamboks. Then he shouted to the people, ordering them to give also to the collection, and before long the space was filled with cattle and sheep and goats, and everywhere there were piles of goods; bowls, soles of sandals, ostrich feathers, leopard skins, and anything else which the people had thought worthy to give.

The very next day the missionaries began their work. At first only a few men were willing to learn and most of them were those who had already attended the missionary school on the Great River while still children, then slowly more and more joined the classes. Garib watched them, torn between eagerness and suspicion, until one day, when he was passing by at a cautious distance from the group for the third time that morning, the Man of God called to him.

"Do you not wish to learn, young man?" he asked.

Once again Garib felt panic and an urgent wish to flee, but already the missionary had him by the arm and was showing him a place to sit next to Kaptein Pieter on the ground beneath the cover of the neat mat roof which had been erected as a school while the mission houses were being built.

At first Garib could not understand. He could make nothing of the strokes and signs the stern White Man was drawing on the strange thing called paper, then he realized that the Man of God was teaching the people how to read the words in the

113

Book and how even to write them for themselves. Garib could see no use for such learning. It filled him with a vague incomprehensible fear, much like the stupefying uneasiness he had felt in the church. Sometimes his fright became so great that his mind sought refuge in blankness and he fell asleep so that the missionary had to shake him to rouse him. But even when Garib did not wish to go to the class in the mornings, something in him seemed to urge him on, and at last, to his own amazement, he too began to recognize words when they were not spoken but only written on paper, and was able to force his hands, so calloused from the tough thongs used on the cattle, to make the right strokes with the thing called a pencil.

Even then the learning was not finished. Every day the men had to repeat long passages after the missionary and learn them by heart. They had to learn the words of sacred songs to the God the missionaries told of and many verses and stories from the Book. They had to know what was called the Ten Commandments and the Catechism and the Lord's Prayer.

But though Garib began to learn all these things he still felt very bewildered by so much strangeness and he continued to muddle the wisdom he was hearing now with the old wisdom Tomarib and his own people had taught him. When he should have been saying, "Our Father which art in Heaven, Hallowed be Thy Name," he found he was thinking, "Thou, O Tsui-Goab! Father of our Fathers! Our Father!" as he had been taught so well as a child.

When he continued in this confusion the missionary had to use his rod across Garib's shoulders to cure him for he said there was only one God and that was Jehovah, the God in the White Man's Book, and then Garib was more confused than ever. He wished to learn, but even now that he could read and write and repeat many passages he could find little meaning in them. He remembered how Tomarib had said that it was through a man's own experience of life that he found the meaning of wise words. He began to despair of ever coming to understand.

Since going to the school Garib had seen even less of Fast Foot than before, but on the evening of the day the Man of

God had used his rod on Garib, Fast Foot found him sitting dejectedly outside his hut and sat down with him to talk.

"*Ai*, Fast Foot," said Garib, "I no longer know even who I am."

"*Eisey!*" exclaimed Fast Foot, wrinkling his forehead in concern. "*A*, Garib, you always have too much eagerness. Leave the school, Young One. What are all these great things to us who are only Men of Men? Come back to your tasks in the cattle fold for this is man's work. *Ai!* These missionaries are as full of words as women!"

Sitting there, Garib saw suddenly that what Fast Foot said was true. He was neglecting his work. He wished more than anything to own a gun and a horse. He would never gain these unless he earned enough sheep and cattle to pay for them. Once before he had tried to learn wisdom from Tomarib and failed. Now he had failed again to understand the wise words the missionaries brought. He gave up going to the school and evaded the eye of the Man of God when attending the church as Haramub ordered. He went back to breaking in ride-oxen in the cattle fold.

And when he was further away from this new confusing wisdom he was able to see more clearly. He saw that, though Haramub himself often took to the pulpit and read from the Book to the people, the wise words had little meaning for him either, and, looking round at the changing town of Ai-gams he began to know why Haramub had asked the Men of God to come to the valley of the Winterhoek. Everywhere the people were learning new ways and growing greater in knowledge. The missionaries taught them how to make bricks for building, and strange candles from tallow to light their huts at night when there was no fire. Under their direction the men of the Warlike People enlarged the gardens and planted pumpkins and mealies and many other crops Garib had never heard of before so that the people did not go hungry in the dry season or sicken from want of vegetables. The Men of God also cleared out the stones and sand from a pool below the springs and after a while many people went to bathe there daily and some of the older women came to like the warm water so much that they sat in the pool most of the day talking and gossiping, and though Fast Foot and some of the other men of the Nama nation who had come to live with Haramub still threw up their hands in horror at the thought of washing, Garib overcame his fear of water and often went to bathe for he still wished to be in every way as superior as the men of Haramub.

Then suddenly one day when Garib was returning up the hill from the bath, a servant of the chief stood before him.

"Master, the chief says that you must come at once to his hut for he has work for a man who is not afraid of lions."

How long Garib had waited for this call! Excited and apprehensive, he followed the servant. Indeed there were more important things than wisdom.

He found the chief sitting in his hut with one of the White Men. There was the same calm satisfied expression on his face which Garib had seen when Haramub had gazed upon the prisoners from Kamoja's tribe which were to strengthen the numbers of his own people. Garib glanced quickly towards the missionary's assistant, then squatted in front of Haramub.

"The White Men tell me you no longer attend school," said the little man.

"No, my chief."

"I do not blame you," said Haramub and Garib breathed more easily. "I have said to the Men of God that they must teach the children. Those who are already men do not learn so quickly. And it is well, Garib Arub, that you are not too busy with your lessons for now I have work for you." He paused. "It is your wish to meet Kahitjene?"

Garib's heart seemed to stop beating with shock, then it began to pound in his chest. For one wild unreasoning moment he thought that the wall of water he had envisaged when he had stood watching Kahitjene's great herds passing along the river bed near Kamoja's village, was about to sweep him into the flood. He thought Haramub was going to tell him, even in front of the White Man, to kill Kahitjene.

Garib took a quick breath. "Yes, my chief," he said, forcing himself to speak bravely.

Haramub smiled. It was an informal, friendly smile and

Garib was amazed to see a kindly pity in the little chief's eyes as if he had read Garib's thoughts.

"I see that too much of the White Man's wisdom has not made you lose your courage, Garib," he said. "That is good for this work I wish you to do asks for a brave man. None of my people are willing to go among the Cattle People for they say the Black Men are too wild and they hate us too much for the things we have done to them. They would kill any of our people if they dared to come near. So now I tell you you must journey with my scout at dawn tomorrow to Kahitjene, for you lived in the house of Kamoja for some time and know the language. You must tell him that the one named Jonker Afrikaner wishes to be his friend. Then you will take this message also to one Tjamuaha who, though not as rich as Kahitjene, is still a chief of many Cattle People. Tell them I wish them to come to Ai-gams so that the White Men may make peace between us."

Garib stared at Haramub, hardly able to believe what he had heard.

"Yes, Garib," said the chief. "The White Men tell me that it will be good to do this thing which their God demands for when there is peace in the land, the traders will come to my town with many articles I require."

"*A, khub,*" whispered Garib.

"And, Garib," said Haramub as he motioned to him to rise. "You know I am a generous man. If you do this thing which I ask I shall not forget you."

"*A, khub,*" said Garib again, and in confusion which was greater even than that which he had felt in the mission school, he went out of the hut. Only one thing was clear to him and that was that at last he was to meet the hated Kahitjene face to face.

Thirteen

Without women and children and cattle to slow their pace, Garib with Haramub's scout and their servants travelled quickly. They went through the stony mountains to the north of Ai-gams, then, keeping close to a low range of hills on their right, crossed the tree-strewn plain beyond until they reached Okahandja, the Place of the Large Flat Sand, where a wide dry river bed wound its way between lofty trees, and where in clearings on the fine ochre-coloured sand the Cattle People had made their homes.

When paths and cattle tracks began to appear, they stopped. With great caution the scout led Garib to a spot from where he could see the lie of the land.

"There!" he whispered, pointing with a finger which was not steady. "To the west under that high hill is the principal village of Kahitjene, and over there on the eastern side at the foot of that high mountain lives his kinsman, Tjamuaha." He looked at Garib fearfully. "It matters little to which chief we travel first for we shall surely be killed wherever we go."

Since his shame in the battle against Kamoja when his terror had caused him to turn to stone, Garib had made it a rule always to do what he feared most first before his courage deserted him. "Lead me to Kahitjene," he said.

In a short while they came out of the bush and Kahitjene's village lay before them. Scattered about among the trees were the homes of the people of the great Cattle King, and wherever Garib looked he could see cattle grazing and people moving about on the paths. Indeed it was as he had thought. Haramub had been willing to risk his life without a qualm for this purpose of his own. Garib's fear was now so great that he dared not hesitate.

He gave the knife he was carrying to the servants and indicated to the scout to hand over his gun likewise so that they might not approach the village armed like enemies. Then they took the feathers of the spotted duck they had brought with them and placed them in their hair, and picked up the unpeeled sticks which among the Men of Men were signs that they had come in peace and not in war.

"Come," said Garib and led the way out into the open.

They were at once in full view of the nearest village. A group of men was standing at the gate but, engrossed in their conversation, they did not notice Garib and the scout. For a longer time than Garib would have believed possible, they walked on in strange safety as if they were somehow invisible.

Then suddenly a child gave a cry. The dogs rushed out barking as they caught the scent of unfamiliar people and the men turned to stare in astonishment.

"It is the yellow hyenas from the south!" screamed a tall woman in a three-eared cap. "It is the men who wear clothing that is like the scum on stagnant water!"

In an instant everyone was running, the women and children towards the bush and the men towards the huts to take up their weapons. "Haramub's people have come to kill us!" they shouted.

Garib and the scout stood as still as stones and waited. Garib licked his lips nervously. Perspiration gathered on his forehead. Then the men, armed with their bows and arrows, their great spears and knobbed clubs, were streaming out of the nearby villages and were gathering outside the gates to defend their homes.

But when Garib and the scout still made no move the Cattle People became confused.

"We come in peace!" shouted Garib in the language of the Black Men. He lifted the unpeeled stick and waved it in the air.

The Cattle People stared at them from a distance. They looked around with great suspicion as if they thought this must surely be a trap and that in a moment the whole forest would come alive with the Warlike People.

119

"We wish to speak with Kahitjene, your chief," called Garib.

The Black Men began to talk among themselves, then at last one of them stepped forward. He was elderly and Garib ·could see from the number of iron beads about his neck that he must be the headman of the village.

"Where are the rest of your people?" the headman shouted. "Where are they hiding with their guns?"

"There are no other men. There are only three servants of the Mountain People tribe in the trees over there."

The Cattle People looked in the direction Garib pointed but there was no one to be seen for the servants had fled in panic when the first shout was given.

Cautiously the tall Black Men came nearer. "They are not armed," said one. "They carry the sticks and feathers of peace," said another.

Soon they were all around the two little Men of Men, touching them, jostling them in growing confidence, and the deep angry sound of their suspicion and displeasure made Garib think back suddenly to a time when, as a child, he had watched a wasp which had been foolish enough to try to enter the nest wild bees had made in a hollow tree. He had seen how the bees had come swarming out to attack the invader and heard their buzzing as they had crowded round, roughly tumbling the wasp as more and ever more bees came to join the angry cluster.

"Kill the thieving dogs!" shouted a young man whose body gleamed and dripped with red ochre and butter. "Kill them! Kill them!" the people took up the chant.

Then suddenly the elderly headman had Garib by the arm and was beating back his men with great blows of his club. "Are you a chief to tell the people what to do?" he shouted at the young man. "Stand back! Stand back! Kahitjene is our chief. We must listen to his voice."

The Cattle People fell back and allowed the headman to lead Garib and the scout towards the nearest village, but their angry murmuring continued as they remembered and spoke of the harm Haramub had done to the Black Men, and Garib knew as he had never known before what it was like to be hated by an enemy people.

The elderly headman kept them in the village for some time while messengers took the news to Kahitjene, then, still surrounded by a dense hostile throng, they were taken along a well-worn path towards the largest of the thorn-fenced homes.

A group of men was waiting outside the Great Hut. All seemed finely dressed and ornately decorated. Then as Garib and the scout reached the hut the group parted quickly and a man came out of the low doorway and stood looking down at Garib and Garib knew at once that this was the man his father had told him to hunt so that blood might pay for blood. He saw with vague surprise that Kahitjene was not young as he had imagined him. His long thin face wore the lines of middle age, but, in spite of this, he was very tall, his dark gleaming body lean and strong and his eyes piercing. Garib saw with surprise too that, unlike most chiefs, Kahitjene was less decorated than his followers. Round his neck was an immense coil of iron beads, so besmeared with red clay that it lay in one solid mass on his chest. Encircling his upper arms were bracelets of valuable white shells which showed him to be a very rich man, and from his waist hung several handsome dagger-knives. But though he wore no rings and bangles about his legs as if he scorned too much ornament, no one with eyes could mistake him for anyone but a chief, for he stood as a man accustomed to respect, his head held well back with pride and dignity and his look bold and fearless.

And when Kahitjene began to speak Garib understood even more how this man could be the greatest Cattle King, the richest and most powerful chief in the country, for he did not waste his breath on useless words. He spoke concisely and well, yet at the same time courteously as if the manners of a chief came naturally to him and he did not need to strive to impress others.

"You come from my neighbour, Haramub of the Warlike People?" he asked.

"Yes, chief," said Garib. "My master who is also called Jonker Afrikaner by the White Men has sent me to ask if you will come to his town to make peace. He sends this message also to one Tjamuaha, the great chief."

Kahitjene listened attentively and it was obvious from the looks he exchanged with the other important men around him that he had already heard this news from the messengers and had spoken of it with his counsellors.

"Why does Jonker Afrikaner wish for peace?" asked Kahitjene. "He has been driving us back with his guns. It is not usual for a man with the sweet taste of triumph in his mouth to ask for peace."

Garib told Kahitjene about the missionaries, explaining as well as he could what such men were and of their God who demanded peace. Some of the Cattle People seemed unable to understand, others doubtful, others openly suspicious. They went aside to discuss matters with their chief, then in a short while returned.

Kahitjene said, "I know nothing of your master, Jonker Afrikaner, but I know that he speaks not only with words but with guns which are more powerful than any weapons my people possess. I know also that I love my cattle above all things and I do not wish to lose them." He spoke with such openness and truthfulness that Garib was amazed. "My herds are not all kept in one place where I may guard them. I have many herds throughout the land wherever there is sufficient grazing for them, and if they are moved from place to place to escape the southern raiders they shall lose their fatness and become thin like the oxen of a poor man."

And the next moment Garib saw that this man who was his sworn enemy was not only truthful but just also, for he said, "And though I know nothing of Haramub I do not condemn him for his victories against my people. He has done nothing which I myself have not done. He has grown rich through battle, even as I have increased the number of my cattle through warfare with clans of the Cattle People who stood against me and with other tribes of the Men of Men. And he has only taken back the land which I and other Cattle Kings took from the Nama peoples in the time of the great drought. So, though I do not fear Jonker Afrikaner, for I fear nothing and no one," and with a growing feeling of awe Garib thought that in this Kahitjene spoke the truth also, "you may tell your master that I am willing to come to speak with him, not as one conquered, but as an equal."

Then he shouted to his women to bring Garib and the scout a dish of thick milk and he told his men to find Garib's servants for he wished to punish them for deserting Haramub's messengers by hanging them in a row from a branch of a tree beside his hut, for they had committed this crime while in his country and this action, he said, would show all men that he meant to be a true friend to Jonker Afrikaner and protect his interests. He said also that already he had sent his own messenger to Tjamuaha's house to the east of Okahandja to summon him and that he would soon arrive.

Garib knew better than to argue against anything the Cattle King said, and when towards evening Tjamuaha arrived he saw that this great chief too knew better than to disagree with Kahitjene. Though Tjamuaha looked at Garib with dislike and suspicion as he passed him and wore a scowl as if he resented being summoned to Kahitjene's house like an inferior chief, when he stood before Kahitjene he showed nothing but courtesy and respect.

He was much more ornately dressed than the Cattle King and his legs below the knees were so ringed with heavy copper bangles that he could only walk with slow dignity. He was almost as tall as Kahitjene, but he did not have the same lordly bearing or fearless expression. His fine narrow eyes had a shrewd look and his face did not display his feelings openly.

"It is good to make peace," he said, "but we should not show too ready a trust in this man Jonker Afrikaner. Let his messenger return to him and tell him that if he wants us to come to his village he must send us his drinking dish and his washing bowl and his knife as pledges of his good faith."

Then Garib knew he had not been wrong in thinking Tjamuaha shrewd. What chief would give over such close possessions to people he meant to deceive? Who would give such power to enemies who might use these things to work magic against him? Yes, this Tjamuaha was a man who would always find a way to ensure his own safety.

"So it shall be," said Kahitjene.

And so it was. When Haramub heard of Tjamuaha's condi-

123

tion to peace, he willingly gave his tin bucket, his tin mug and his knife. Garib saw that his fear of witchcraft was not as strong as that of the people of Arub or the Black Men. He told Garib to take these possessions quickly and bring Tjamuaha and Kahitjene back with him for he could obtain more and finer goods from the traders very easily when they arrived.

And when all was completed Garib was at last able to bring the two great chiefs of the Cattle People to Ai-gams together with many of their important men. They arrived on the night before the great feast day which the missionaries had told them was called Christmas and which was the celebration of the day on which the Son of God, Jesus, of whom they spoke so often, was born into the world.

As they came up the hill below the hot springs the people of Haramub watched them in silent suspicion but they made no move to oppose them and Garib saw that many of them wished earnestly for this peace so that they could live without fear of attack.

The next day all the people of Haramub gathered in the church and Haramub himself took the pulpit.

"The people who walked in darkness," he read from the Book at the place opened for him, "have seen a great light; light has dawned upon them, dwellers in a land as dark as death. Thou hast increased their joy and given them great gladness; they rejoice in thy presence as men rejoice at harvest, or as they are glad when they share out the spoil; for thou hast shattered the yoke that burdened them, the collar that lay heavy on their shoulders. All the boots of trampling soldiers and the garments fouled with blood shall become a burning mass, fuel for fire. For unto us a child is born, unto us a son is given: and the government shall be upon his shoulder: and his name shall be called Wonderful, Counsellor, The Mighty God, The Everlasting Father, The Prince of Peace!"

Then the missionary with the steady solemn gaze cried out, "Today we see the fulfilment of the law that all men shall love one another. Our God is a God of peace. Live in peace and the God of Love and Peace shall be with you, and it is written also, 'Blessed are the peacemakers for they shall be called the children of God.'"

And after the service, while Haramub, Tjamuaha and
Kahitjene sat in the house of the missionaries, drinking the
White Men's drink called tea and making their promises of
peace and friendship, Garib and the rest of the people of
Ai-gams took the other Cattle Men to the place where fires for
roasting had been made and a feast had been laid out on mats
upon the ground.

At first the Men of Men were very ill-at-ease to find themselves suddenly in such close company with the tall Black Men
who were so different from themselves and whom they had
always regarded as enemies to be feared and hated. The Cattle
People too seemed shy and suspicious and kept together in a
group as if they found it difficult to believe their chiefs who
had ordered them to show friendship. But as the honey beer
was passed round and the Men of Men began to mingle with
the Black Men to offer them long strips of roast meat still
dripping with fat and juices from the fire, their stomachs
were warmed and both nations were able to relax, and soon,
though some eyes still showed mistrust, the crowd as a whole
seemed pleased and in good spirits. They could not speak
the same language, but they could smile, and the more the
people mingled, the gayer they became until their laughter
could be heard throughout the town and Garib saw that men
did not need a common tongue when they spoke in friendship.

And as Garib moved among the Cattle Men, eating and
drinking with them, he became aware of a strange feeling of
contentment growing within him, and listening to their merriment he thought of how different was the sound of friendship
to the angry buzzing of a hostile enemy.

What had the missionaries said? Blessed are the peacemakers. He realized that Tomarib had been right when he
had said a man could learn the meaning of wise words only
through his experience of life. He remembered how he had
pondered on the strangeness that when a man hurt another
he felt the pain in his own body. Now he saw that even though
Haramub's reasons for seeking peace were not those the Men
of God wished for, when men showed friendship to others
they themselves could feel joy. And though he still could not
understand how people who were not of the same kind might

125

love one another as the missionary said, he could see, through his experience of this feast, that when men of different nations came together as friends it gave them happiness, and when they sat together and shared food and drink in peace, it was very good.

Fourteen

There was a saying among the Cattle People: Two things make a great chief; a large number of cattle and a numerous following of men. It was as if Haramub too believed in this wisdom for no sooner had he made peace with the Black Men than he began earnestly to strengthen his tribe. He already had plenty of cattle; the valleys were filled with them. Now he set about increasing the number of his followers.

He asked Tjamuaha and Kahitjene to move their homes to the Winterhoek so that they might be nearer to him in case the large tribes of Cattle People to the north, with whom he had made no peace, attacked suddenly, and Tjamuaha and Kahitjene, to show their good faith came with some of their cattle and built their separate villages near to Ai-gams.

Then Haramub sent word to his relations who still remained along the Great River in the south, and these people, hearing of the growing prosperity of Ai-gams, came eagerly to join the little chief.

And Haramub's men, watching all these people arriving with their belongings to enjoy the shelter of the Winterhoek began to say, "Indeed our chief means to keep this peace. He has forgotten his great boasts. Now he has kept the promise he made to Games. He has driven back the Cattle People to their own country. Honour is satisfied."

Soon other people also began to believe that the peace was real. The little black Mountain People came down in their hundreds from the barren hills where they had been hiding in fear from the fierce Black Men and asked Haramub to allow them to be servants in his town. And in addition many adventurers from all the Nama tribes came to join Haramub and lived on the western side of the mountains.

Garib watched the growth of Ai-gams with interest and amazement. The greatness he longed for seemed very close. Haramub remembered his promise to reward him. He gave him the gun and the horse he had desired for so long and ordered him to move out of the hut of the herdsmen into a hut of his own nearer to the other important men of the tribe.

And at the end of the next season of summer, when the dust lay on the hills, the traders arrived, and then the town went wild with excitement. The White Men came with their wagons laden with goods, some of which even the people of Ai-gams had never seen, and set up shop under their big carts. There were gaily coloured shawls and red handkerchiefs, beads, shining knives, tinderboxes with which men could make fires, clothing and bright materials for the women to turn into skirts and dresses such as the missionaries' wives wore. They were all temptingly displayed and the people were so overwhelmed by the sight of these splendid things that they clamoured to obtain them. The women begged shrilly for their husbands to buy handkerchiefs for their heads and striped petticoats and shawls and beads and the many strange foods which they had not tasted since leaving the Great River. From out of skin and canvas bags tied to the sides of the wagons came sugar, tea, coffee, rice and dried peas.

Haramub had first choice of all the goods. For a whole herd of fat oxen he bought guns, and bullets in pouches, and powder horns, and flints and choppers and many strange tools for working wood and iron. Then for another herd he bought himself, his fine large wife and his sons and daughters, clothing of all description and new pots and kettles.

The trader was very pleased. "I see we shall be good friends," he called out in Dutch. "You have the cattle and we have the goods. We shall make good use of the road you built over the mountains." Then, still laughing, the White Man bent down and handed a strange-looking vessel to Haramub's servant who was collecting the purchases. "Give this to your master as a present for being such a good customer."

Garib did not know what the present was, but Kaptein Pieter told him later that it was one of the White Men's drinks, but it was not tea. It was called brandy and the vessel it came in was named a bottle.

Then the other men crowded forward. Kaptein Pieter gave a slaughter cow from his own herd for a shirt and a handkerchief, and Hendrick gave a sheep for a fine new hat, and Garib was so bewildered that when his turn came, he pushed his ox forward but could not remember the names of the new goods. Kaptein Pieter had to come to his aid and amid much laughter and merriment the great Kaptein bought him not only a shirt but a sunshade of pink cloth and a bag of peas as well.

From then on the appearance of Ai-gams changed rapidly. A blacksmith came to live there and began to put old guns into order and forge new weapons and make all kinds of iron articles. Ox-wagons and carts became common sights in the streets. Old skin clothing almost disappeared and all people who respected themselves, even Fast Foot, went about in White Men's clothes. Even the Nama tribesmen on the western hills became wearers of hats and started to wash their bodies and called themselves proudly civilized persons. Everywhere iron pots and shiny kettles were to be seen and the women sat all morning at the hot springs filling their new tea pots with hot water and drinking the White Men's beverage in preference to sour milk, and many men even ceased to sit upon the ground and bought chairs from the traders and carried them about with them when they went to visit a neighbour.

Then Haramub, watching his town grow with much pride told the people that they must no longer call him Haramub, but must use his White Man's name, Jonker Afrikaner, for he intended to live like a White Man. And then all the people remembered again the names they had been given in the south.

"You too must have a proper name," Haramub said to Garib. "Garib Arub is an offence to the tongue. I shall call you David."

"Yes, my chief," said Garib. David, David, he thought, trying to learn this new word by heart and finding it very strange and somewhat frightening. He had been taught as a child that a man's name had great power and must not be used carelessly lest spirits hear it spoken and use it to work evil. He told of this fear to no one for he knew that his own people had been ignorant of many things and this must surely be just another superstition, but nevertheless he was uneasy. For a long time, in the rapidly changing scene, he had hardly known who he was, and if a man changed his name then might he not perhaps lose himself altogether?

But as Garib looked about Ai-gams he saw that Jonker Afrikaner was right to call him David. The old possessions and old ways could find little place in this great new town. The traders paid many visits and brought with them many wonderful luxuries for the people. Jonker Afrikaner's son, Christian Afrikaner, who would one day be chief in Haramub's place wore a fine coat of red cloth, and all the important women went about dressed in long flowing skirts of bright material with gay handkerchiefs tied about their heads, and in the heat of the day delicate sunshades of many colours could be seen everywhere between the huts. And more than this, every time the White Men came they brought more brandy.

Then the chief went himself back with the traders to the harbour on the coast to arrange for more goods to be sent to Ai-gams. Garib stood with the other people by the springs to cheer him on his way. He watched Jonker Afrikaner climb on to the wagon in a fine new red coat and new trousers and White Men's shoes. He was no longer slim as a lathe. His prosperity had caused him to put on weight so that his movements were slower and more dignified. He was an impressive sight.

Garib was there again when at length the chief returned with the White Men. He watched Haramub climbing down from the wagon and gasped in alarm as the little man lurched and almost lost his balance. He knew at once there was something wrong. The chief must be ill. He elbowed his way forward until he could see. Then he stopped. Haramub's face was flushed and his gait unsteady, but it was not caused by fever. Jonker Afrikaner was drunk.

Garib's mouth opened in astonishment. He had seen other men drunk many times with hemp and honey beer, but never before had he known Haramub to behave with foolishness. Haramub had always been the one to keep others in order with uncompromising strictness.

Then Jonker Afrikaner turned and saw Garib.

"Eisey!" he cried, stumbling towards him and clutching at his arm. "It is the Lion-killer! So, Garib!" he went on, leaning on Garib and breathing brandy fumes into his face. "But I must not call you Garib, must I? You are David, my man David who is not afraid of lions." He laughed but it was not a pleasant sound.

"But do not fear, David," he said, letting Garib go and standing beside him swaying slightly. "I shall make you great. Have I not already made my people great?" He pointed to the wagon laden with more goods. "Who can say now that we are lower than baboons and worse than dogs? Now the White Men do not dare to scorn me for I am too important. Now they are my friends. Did they not tell me this while they drank with me?"

Garib looked at the trader who was still seated on the wagon and saw that he was grinning, and he realized with a shock that was followed quickly by anger that these White Men were not like the Men of God. It was not friendship that caused them to drink with Haramub but greed for his wealth. And Haramub's words made Garib remember how, on their arrival in the Winterhoek, the little chief had, in an unguarded moment, let him glimpse the wound the scorn of the White Men in the south had caused, and which, it had seemed to him, still lay unhealed and festering in some hidden place inside him. Acceptance could heal a wound, but Jonker Afrikaner would not find it among these traders. *Ai!* Some of these White Men were no better than white Bushmen!

He stared after Haramub as he walked uncertainly towards his house with his Elders, a bottle of brandy still in his hand. And that night as Garib lay alone in his important hut the uneasiness which he had felt since the coming of the missionaries changed into fearful apprehension for he did not know what a wounded beast might do when it drank the White Men's brandy.

Fifteen

Garib's anxiety at the sudden change in Haramub was so great that before he was even fully awake the next morning he was aware of a depressing sense of dread, and when he came out into the busy roadway he almost expected to find the whole town fallen and destroyed. It was Haramub's energy and Haramub's vision which had brought Ai-gams into being. How could it continue to exist in splendour when its maker had tottered? But in the fresh early morning light the town looked just as usual. Men were washing in their tin buckets outside their doors, and women in bright dresses were returning from the hot springs with their teapots, and everywhere children, some naked, some dressed in White Men's materials, were running and shouting happily.

And when he saw Jonker Afrikaner a little later outside his hut Garib was able to shrug off most of his apprehension, for apart from a redness of the eyes and an irritable expression, the chief looked just as usual also, and, as if he had read with annoyance the uncertainty in other faces besides Garib's he called all his important men together in council and told them of his new plan to form his Cattle People friends into fighting units.

"They shall be formed into sections with Tjamuaha's son, Maherero, as their Kaptein and they shall all be under my command."

Several of the Elders at once began to speak out against this plan for they said it was foolishness to put such strength into the hands of people who had so short a while before been their bitter enemies, but Jonker Afrikaner, as if still determined to prove that the brandy had not weakened his strength, refused to listen. For the first time Garib saw the little chief lose his temper.

"It shall be as I say!" shouted Jonker Afrikaner. "Do you think I am a fool? Indeed I would be a fool if I listened to what you say! Tjamuaha and Kahitjene live in my valley. They dig for the roots which my people should eat and their cattle graze off my pastures, and they must be of use to me. There are still many thousands of Black Men in the north who have no love for me and I mean to wrap my new allies about me as a fruit wraps the peel about it to protect its juices. Tjamuaha and Kahitjene shall stand between me and my enemies!"

Not even the chief Elders dared to argue when they saw the anger in Haramub's hard eyes, and, as always, the chief lost no time in putting a scheme into practice. Before long the sound of the young Black Men stamping and singing as they performed their war-dances in obedience to Jonker Afrikaner's command could be heard lower down the valley.

And indeed though Garib saw the chief helpless with intoxication several times after that there was still no sign that he was losing his control over his people. Instead he seemed to be growing greater. The valley of the Winterhoek became a centre for trading, the like of which the country had never seen. Namas and Cattle People and even Mountain People came from the hills all around to barter with each other for cattle, rings, axes and spearheads as they had never been able to do before, and the White traders kept arriving with wagons so heavily loaded that they stuck fast in the pale sand. Soon Jonker Afrikaner owned everything the White Men could bring him. He even possessed many carts and wagons of his own and was able to make his own bullets with the moulds the traders sold him. And in exchange for all these goods enormous herds of Haramub's cattle were constantly being taken out of the country, driven by the traders across the mountains and over the plains towards the Cape.

So life in Ai-gams settled down into its new pattern. In every way the people tried to become more and more like the White Men and Garib saw that they were beginning to be ashamed of being Men of Men. Now if they wished to dance they went to a place beyond the gaze of the missionaries, and no one would have thought of going to church in skin clothing.

Instead the men wore every kind of garment with which the traders had been able to supply them. Most wore broad-brimmed hats of coarse material and dark coats and trousers, but some, who had been wealthy enough to afford the price of gayer clothing, came garbed in long-tailed coats that reached below their knees and tall shiny hats that sat like round boxes upon their heads, and some even more fortunate wore the scarlet uniforms which the traders told the people were worn by the White soldiers in the south.

The women came to services looking just as impressive. Their dresses were of brilliant cloth and each one had her head bound up with great care with three handkerchiefs of different colours, so adjusted as to show the colour of each.

And not only were they different now in their dress but also in their behaviour in church. Few people wept now or had to be carried away when the missionaries read from the Book. Instead so many of them got into the habit of falling asleep during the prayers that Haramub appointed messengers to walk about the building to rouse any sleepers with a great blow upon their heads.

But no one paid heed to these small differences. Even when the missionaries ceased to speak so much of the love of God and shouted out instead passages from the Book which told of the terrible destruction awaiting those who did not keep the Word, they took little notice. The prosperity all around them was so great that it blinded the eye to all else.

There were several other things of a less pleasant nature which they chose not to see also. Since the beginning of time people in this land of drought and sparse pasturage had had to live a wandering existence, for wherever men settled in any numbers the grazing was soon eaten off by sheep and cattle. Now too many men with too many cattle had been living too long in the valley of the Winterhoek. The herdsmen had to take Haramub's herds further and further away to find sufficient grass for them, and, more than this, there was no game left for it had all been killed or had fled from the hunters' guns. And with so many people searching for food all

134

the roots and bulbs had disappeared from the ground. For a great distance all around Ai-gams there was no blade of grass or edible bulb.

But Haramub's people did not worry. They had always lived mainly on the meat from their great herds of captured cattle, and whatever else they needed could be had by bartering still more beasts with the traders. It had never been in the nature of the Men of Men to live, even in thought, in any time except the present, and when the present was sweet what cause was there to think of anything else. Haramub had always been an exception, but now even he seemed satisfied with this unbelievable prosperity. What man on earth could ask for more?

And so while they were well fed and had everything they desired they were not troubled too much by the impoverished state of the many Namas who had gathered on the western slopes in the hopes of sharing in Haramub's glory. Hungry, with few cattle left to barter, and jealous of the wealth of the Warlike People, they began to steal one or two beasts from the vast herds of Tjamuaha and Kahitjene which grazed so temptingly within their reach.

"Yes, yes," said Jonker Afrikaner when the Cattle Kings reported these crimes. "The thieves shall be punished." But it was as if the little chief too was blinded by fine living for the culprits were never caught.

And it was not only the adventurers on the western slopes that were envious of the Warlike People. The Nama tribes further south were also watching with greedy eyes. By now Games the queen was dead and Oasib was chief in her place. He hated Haramub for he saw how the little man had snatched the power from him, and he begrudged his new wealth. Determined to gain at least a small share in so much success, Oasib and his men advanced on Ai-gams. But Oasib was a chief who prided himself on his cleverness. He dared not attack Jonker Afrikaner himself so he paid a friendly visit to Kahitjene instead. It was dusk and Kahitjene, hearing of their arrival and mindful of his manners as a chief, sent messengers to his village where they were waiting to tell his people to show his friends, the Men of Men, every kindness. Calabashes of milk were at once served to Oasib and his men, and when they had refreshed themselves they suddenly turned on their generous hosts and, after killing all those who offered any resistance, drove off all of Kahitjene's cattle which were being cared for by the village and disappeared into the night before anyone could stop them.

In a fury Kahitjene sent messengers to Jonker Afrikaner the next morning.

"My chief says that they are your people and this is your country," said the tall arrogant Black Man who carried Kahitjene's words. "He says it is your work to punish them."

The people in Ai-gams listened to the news in surprise and apprehension and, looking round, Garib saw that, in spite of their greatness the Warlike People had not lost their fear of the big Cattle People.

But as the messengers walked away Jonker Afrikaner said, "Am I to be ordered by dogs?" Then with the quick irritation he so often showed now in the morning after he had been drinking with his Kapteins, he added, "This Kahitjene seems to forget who is master in this valley."

For six days the people of Ai-gams waited, but still their chief made no move to go after the robbers, and on the seventh day the people fled in panic from the hot springs for a large crowd of Cattle Men were approaching Ai-gams along the road. But as they came closer it was seen that they did not come in war for they carried no weapons.

In angry silence the tall Black Men went to Haramub's hut and when Haramub came out to hear their complaint, Kahitjene stepped forward. Garib had not seen much of the Cattle King since his coming to the Winterhoek and once again he was overawed by the big man's dignity and boldness.

"Chief of the Warlike People!" said Kahitjene, and even though he and his men were unarmed and all around them Jonker Afrikaner's people were standing ready with their guns, he still showed no fear. "I have come to tell you this. When those whom you call Cattle People trade with others they barter with caution. If a man gives an ox for an axe in fair exchange, on returning home he will examine the axe carefully, sitting all day looking at it. And if at last he finds a flaw in the metal he will immediately bring it back to the man from whom he obtained it, throw it down at his feet and take back his own ox without speaking a word."

He stopped and looked Haramub straight in the face and Garib noticed that it was the little chief who looked away in discomfort.

"And I have come to say that for many moons I have been examining this friendship which you gave to me in exchange for my young men to protect your town. I see now there are many flaws in it for your people continually steal my cattle and you do nothing to support me. So now I have not come to quarrel with you, but only to return to you what is yours and to take back what is rightfully mine. Here is your friendship," he said, moving his empty hand as if he were tossing something at Haramub's feet. "I am now on my way with my young men and the rest of my people back to my home in Okahandja." And without uttering another word or even waiting for Jonker Afrikaner to speak, Kahitjene turned and went back down the hill.

The little chief watched him go. His face was expressionless. He was silent until the tall gleaming Black Men had disappeared from view, then he looked away.

"Let them go," he said carelessly to the men around him. "This valley is too full of people," and he went into his hut.

"Haramub does not care if the Cattle King chooses to leave," said the man next to Garib.

But Garib knew he was wrong. He had seen in Haramub's narrow eyes that look of cold ruthlessness, which he had learnt to respect with awe, and he knew that the chief *did* care. And he knew too that he was no longer alone in his hatred of the Cattle King who had brought such grief to his people. In scorning Jonker Afrikaner, Kahitjene had, without intention, made a second and far more deadly enemy.

Sixteen

As soon as Tjamuaha heard the news of Kahitjene's departure he came hurrying to Ai-gams with his important people and his son, Maherero.

"O Great Chief!" he said to Jonker Afrikaner. "I am come to assure you of my continued friendship lest you think that I, like Kahitjene, will desert you. But I tell you this is not so. I am not as proud or as hasty as the Cattle King. What reason have I for breaking the peace? Am I not far better off here with you than I was previously. Here my cattle are safe from attack by my jealous kinsmen. In this sheltered valley they shall increase until I too am a great Cattle King."

All the while Tjamuaha was making this long speech Jonker Afrikaner sat upon his stool outside his hut and listened in silence. And Tjamuaha, seeing that the little chief showed no great desire to hear his words, became even louder in his protestations of loyalty, and Garib felt a vague pity for him for he saw scorn openly displayed on several of the faces of Haramub's people. The Men of Men were not fools. They knew well enough that Tjamuaha had no choice now but to stay near Jonker Afrikaner for he was not powerful like Kahitjene. If he went away from Haramub's protection the Cattle People in the north would soon destroy him.

"Great Chief!" shouted Tjamuaha. "I too have come to tell you of a custom among the Black Men. When one tribe wishes to make peace with another, the chief goes to the leader of the other people and gives him a lean calf, and it is understood that as long as the calf lives, so long shall his promise of friendship continue. So I have come to show you my great desire for friendship. I have brought you my son to live in

138

your house." He led his tall fine son and heir, Maherero, forward. "He shall be the calf of peace between us."

Jonker Afrikaner gazed at Tjamuaha thoughtfully, then at Maherero, and he was so long in answering to accept Tjamuaha's offer that Garib thought he meant to reject it with silence. Then the little chief spoke and his tone was as careless as it had been when speaking of Kahitjene. "This is a good calf, Tjamuaha," he said. "As long as you obey me and prove your friendship in assisting me in all ways, you may stay in this valley."

The words were so abrupt that a dark look of anger and resentment passed over Tjamuaha's long thin face, but he realized the weakness of his position too well to protest further. He looked down slowly. "It is as you say, O Chief," he said. "As long as my son lives, I shall be your friend."

But though Tjamuaha called himself a friend and though he towered above Haramub as a giraffe-thorn tree towers above the bush at its feet, Garib saw now quite clearly that the time of friendship was over, and in this new alliance Tjamuaha was no longer an equal, but a servant to do his master's bidding.

But like a flower which is picked, yet still keeps its appearance of freshness for some while, peace continued in the land as if it still lived. Then, as a brown stain begins to appear on plucked petals, the prosperity gained through peace showed signs of tarnish. The silks and satins of the women's clothes were no longer so gay and bright as they had been when new. The garments began to look dirty and torn, paper and rubbish lay unheeded in the streets, and, as if the people took their example from their chief, many of the men developed a great liking for the White Men's brandy, and when brandy could not be had they quenched their thirst with ever increasing amounts of intoxicating honey beer, and now Jonker Afrikaner no longer checked them, for his own craving had become too great.

Instead of punishing men who were drunk or disorderly, he built another stone house, like the church, and made it into a place where cheap beer could be brewed from honey and wild raisins. Soon Tjamuaha's people too developed a taste for this sweet honey beer and wild living became the order of the day. In a short while all the raisin bushes around Ai-gams had been stripped of their small sweet fruit and all the bees' nests robbed of their honey. This made Jonker Afrikaner angry for he saw with an anxious eye how the great herds that were being given over to the traders were still leaving his valley, and he did not wish his people to waste good beasts in payment for brandy when honey beer did almost as well. He ordered his people to tie strips of rag torn from old shirts and petticoats to the raisin bushes as tokens of ownership, according to the ancient custom of the Men of Men. And when this did not help and the big footprints of the Cattle People were still found around the bushes, he called for Garib.

"Bind my friend's calf to the wagon wheel for three days," he said, and Garib had to tie Maherero to the wheel of one of the chief's wagons with leather thongs. "Tjamuaha must learn that when Jonker Afrikaner speaks, his friend must listen."

But still the peace continued and though Haramub no longer ordered his people to go to church, or went himself, many continued to attend services and heard the missionaries' warnings and rebukes. By now the first Men of God had left and new missionaries had taken their place and built a mission station close to Ai-gams, but what they said was the same.

"Hold fast that which is good!" they cried. "Abstain from all appearance of evil!"

And when they saw that many of the people did not listen but hid those things from them which they preached against, they would not shake hands with the offenders or allow them to be members of the church, and they reprimanded the beer drinkers and told the women of the evils of drinking too much tea, and beat any man who wished to have two wives with a strap until he admitted his error.

The more the Men of God tried to force Jonker Afrikaner's people to keep the withering peace, the less they seemed to obey, and some of them became insolent, even firing their guns when they heard the church bell ringing, and others refused to give to the collection at the end of the service.

Garib watched all this happening and he was glad when he

saw how strict and difficult the Men of God were becoming that he had not stayed longer at the mission school, and he was more convinced than ever that their wisdom, like Tomarib's, had little meaning, but he felt dissatisfied. He wandered round the town restlessly. He had no desire for honey beer for he saw how foolish and pitiful men became when intoxicated. His own dream of glory was still too strong to allow him to take this path. He yearned instead for Haramub to rouse himself so that the chief might give him tasks more fitting to a man than tying Maherero to the wheel.

"I have this restless feeling because I have not yet done as my father ordered me," Garib told himself. "Only when I have killed Kahitjene will I know that I am indeed a man worthy of manhood." And as he watched the flower of peace fading and dying, he felt the old excitement stirring. Haramub had said that he must not hunt the jackal that was Kahitjene until he gave the word. Now the Cattle King was Haramub's enemy as well as Garib's. It could not be long before Jonker Afrikaner awoke from sleep.

And as if to hasten Haramub's awakening, the locusts came. The hoppers came down from the north like an army, crawling and hopping across the plains under a scorching summer sun. Hissing, rustling and chirruping, bumping, tumbling and jostling, they advanced slowly southward towards Ai-gams in great reddish-brown masses.

Then, gaining the full strength of their wings, the locusts took to the air. When they reached the mountains sheltering the Winterhoek valley they rose abruptly in compact bodies as if propelled by strong gusts of air and settled again on the other side.

Whirling and swirling, rising and falling like clouds of red dust, the locusts came down the valley. At first the noise they made was like a droning hum, then as they came nearer it was like a gale of wind whistling through the leaves of a giraffe-thorn forest. And still the clouds grew larger and larger until, coming between the earth and the sun, they darkened the air and their sound was like that of a raging storm.

With shouts of joy the people of Ai-gams rushed out to meet the locusts, eager for the taste of the fat juicy insects.

They leapt and pranced under the shimmering haze of vibrat-ing wings while the locusts fell thickly about them like dry leaves. They put large quantities of wood in the path of the swarm and lit it and as the insects passed over the fire their wings were scorched and they fell helplessly to the ground. The people scooped them up in every dish and bucket and collected whole cartloads for their feast, and in the evening, when the sheepskin karosses had been laid round the fire, they ate the roasted locusts by the handful, munching and crushing and sucking in the sharp, bitter taste.

And after the locusts were gone there was no blade of grass or green bush to be seen anywhere. There were only great patches of bare ground and leafless trees, as if a fire had scorched the earth. Even the mat huts over which they had passed were picked to the frames. There were no fruits or berries left, no pasturage for the cattle anywhere in the Winterhoek. The people called it the famine year.

Shortly afterwards the traders' wagons arrived once again in Ai-gams. The people crowded round to watch the bartering, but the White Men would not put out their goods for them to see.

"What is the matter?" Garib asked Kaptein Pieter who had been called out to beat back those who tried to be too importunate.

"The chief has no more cattle to use in exchange."

"No more cattle!" For many seasons now the bulk of Hara-mub's beasts had been grazed at some distance from the town wherever there was pasturage, and Garib had had no idea how quickly the herds of captured cattle, which had seemed inexhaustible, had been spent on silks and satins and brandy.

"*Eisey!*" exclaimed Kaptein Pieter. "And it is even worse than that. The chief owes the traders eight hundred head of cattle and as many sheep and goats and the traders say they cannot part with any more goods until he can pay the debt."

For a long while the traders and Jonker Afrikaner and his Elders were shut away in the chief's hut, then the White Men went away and later that day messengers came running down the road. They fetched Haramub's brother and Kaptein Pieter and several others who were Kapteins of the army and Garib waited, but he was not called.

Burning with curiosity and impatience, he watched for Kaptein Pieter to return, and when he did he beckoned to him.

"Why is the chief calling together the men?" he asked.

Kaptein Pieter grinned. "How do I know?" he said. "The chief says we are to go hunting in the north with Maherero and his men."

"Hunting!"

"Yes," said Kaptein Pieter, but the old wicked gleam of amusement was in his eye for he knew as well as Garib that there were few wild creatures left in the valleys and even the ostriches were so hunted that it was impossible to come within range of them with a gun. The game they were going to hunt was the fat cattle of the Black Men.

The peace was broken. The fallen flower, its beauty gone, had laid for long unheeded upon the ground, and now Jonker Afrikaner, in his need, was about to trample it into the dust beneath the heel of his White Men's boot.

Seventeen

When Jonker Afrikaner and the "hunters" returned, they brought with them four thousand head of cattle, and when the people saw them coming along the road, they rushed out to meet them with excited cries of praise, just as they had in the time of Haramub's great victories. And in a flurry of dust and clatter of hooves, the men who had gained this prize came riding into Ai-gams with triumphant shouts and great swelling boasts. Everything was just as it had been in the old days when the Warlike People had known themselves to be superior to all others because of the sweet taste of success in their mouths.

And once again there were cattle in plenty for barter. Jonker Afrikaner and his men chose all the best beasts for themselves and gave the rest to Tjamuaha to share among his people. Once more the traders' wagons came over the mountain and everyone was happy.

It was only when the missionaries with grave faces stood among them that the people lost their smiles, but Haramub spoke out loudly in their defence. "We are innocent people," he said. "We went to the north only to punish wrongdoers who were breaking the peace with tribal warfare. These beasts are our just payment."

And Garib knew that Jonker Afrikaner longed to punish Kahitjene also for his insult. But though Haramub watched the Cattle King from a distance, as a leopard, hidden among the branches of a thicket, watches the movements of his prey, he did not attack him openly. Instead, on the pretext once more of keeping order in the land, he attacked a chief of a small unimportant clan who was Kahitjene's half-brother and killed him and sixty of his followers.

When Garib heard this news he felt his throat tighten with excitement for he knew that among the Cattle People there was the same ancient law regarding revenge as existed among the Men of Men. When a man was killed it was the sacred duty of his nearest kin to avenge his death. With the stealth and cleverness of the great cat he resembled, Jonker Afrikaner had rustled the leaves to betray his presence, and like a baited lion, Kahitjene fell upon Haramub and his horsemen when they were returning from a visit to the harbour and in a terrible battle was defeated.

Hardly able to believe the rumours which reached Ai-gams, Garib rode out to meet his chief.

Jonker Afrikaner's face was flushed with triumph and when he saw Garib he reined in his horse. "So, David!" he shouted. "Men thought Kahitjene was a lion, but he was nothing but a jackal after all. He tried to attack us and we defeated him. But we did not kill him. He has run into the bush with his tail between his legs, and one day soon I shall call you to hunt this low beast for I have not forgotten how you long for his blood."

But when Garib spoke about the battle to Kaptein Pieter he learnt that it had not gone as easily as Jonker Afrikaner would have him believe. The Cattle King and his men, armed only with spears and bows and arrows, had fought with great fierceness and killed some of Haramub's men and even wounded the little chief's son, Christian Afrikaner, and though Kahitjene had fled he was still a powerful man and one to be reckoned with.

"If we had not had horses and guns it might have gone badly with us, David," the Kaptein admitted, and remembering the Kaptein's quick battle against Kamoja, Garib realized that no matter how brave and strong a chief might be, there were no people who could stand against the White Men's weapons. And Tjamuaha seemed to understand this also for he kept quite quiet and did not even rebuke Jonker Afrikaner for defeating his kinsman.

Only the Men of God dared to rebuke the little chief. "You must shun the ways of unrighteousness and avoid committing acts which, unless they are repented of, will cause you to forfeit the kingdom of heaven. If you raid and steal cattle, sin will lie at your door."

"Sin?" said Haramub, frowning as if he did not like the missionary's words. "We fought only to defend ourselves. And if we have taken a few cattle when passing through the country we have still left plenty behind us."

The Man of God did not move. He continued to stare down at Haramub as he sat with his Elders outside his hut. "Jehovah is a God of Peace," he said. "If you do not keep his commandments you will perish with all the kingdom of evil and be utterly destroyed in the fires of Hell."

Anger came quickly into Haramub's small triangular face. "You talk so much of God," he said. "Who has seen this God? And where is Hell? Who has returned from there to tell you of its fires? I do not believe there is such a place."

Shaking their heads, the missionaries went away, and after that Haramub no longer made any pretence of keeping the peace. In the blacksmith's shop bullets and spear heads were made as quickly as it was possible to make them, and guns were put into order and every preparation was made for open warfare, and like a veld fire spreading across the plains in the time of dryness, the word went out to the tribes in the south. "The peace is broken. We may once more hunt the cattle of the Black Men."

At once Oasib, senior chief of the Nama nation, and many other Nama clans eager for a share in the riches, came up from the south. By now many of them too possessed guns and horses, purchased from the traders, and with the greatest of ease they attacked the smaller villages, beat back the people, rounded up the cattle and disappeared back into the south. And to make up for their losses, one clan of Cattle Men turned against the next.

Everywhere there was fighting and all around Ai-gams unruly bands of armed Men of Men hid in the mountains waiting to make further raids, and on a journey to check the safety of one of Haramub's cattle outposts Garib encountered one of these bands.

They rushed out at him from their hiding place in the

146

bushes and Garib, thinking they meant to rob him, quickly snatched his gun from under his arm and prepared to defend himself.

In a moment they had surrounded his horse, but they made no move to molest him. Garib looked down at them suspiciously. He had never before seen such a dirty tattered crowd of people. Some wore leather trousers and coats without shirts, others still wore loinskins under long jackets, and all had hats of different types on their heads with gaudy red ribbons round them which told Garib that they were some of Oasib's men.

Then the leader, a middle-aged man with a thin sharp face and narrow cruel eyes, spoke. "Do not shoot, man of the Warlike People. We are friends."

There was something so familiar in his harsh tone that Garib looked at him again. It was Arub the Big One. Quickly his gaze searched among the rest of the crowd, but he could recognize none of the others. He realized then how much he himself must have changed for it was many seasons since he had been a boy in the house of Arub.

"Do you not know me?" he asked. "I am Garib, son of Arub the Hunter."

The Big One looked at him in astonishment, then staring up fiercely at Garib and seeing that the young man had spoken truly, cried out, "Son of my brother! Indeed you have grown great! We thought you had long since been killed by the Cattle People!"

Garib moved uneasily. He was revolted by Arub's appearance and longed to spur his horse on, but suddenly he knew that there was one question which he must ask for it was a matter which had worried him much.

"Big One," he said. "How is my mother? Does she still live?"

"Indeed she is well, my son," said Arub, eyeing Garib's fine saddle greedily. "She is now living with what is left of our people at the Great Place of Oasib at Hoachanas. *Eisey*, Garib, the house of Arub is no longer a separate clan but has been eaten up by Oasib's tribe. Your sister is there too and is grown into a fine young woman. But come to my camp. It is not far

147

and I can tell you much. Yes, come, Garib," he added with a sly look as if he had just thought of some advantage which might be gained from this unexpected meeting. He moved closer and raised his arm as if to touch Garib.

Without thinking, Garib recoiled. He pulled at the rein so that his horse whinnied, tossing its head.

"No, Arub," Garib called desperately. "That I cannot do for I am now one of Jonker Afrikaner's men and I have urgent work to do for him."

Without looking back, Garib urged his horse on to a brisk trot and in a short while he had left Arub and his band behind. He remembered what Kahitjene's people had called those who wore White Men's clothing, and Arub the Big One and those with him were indeed like the scum which forms on dirty water. He had no wish to see any more of them. *Eisey!* he thought, shuddering. He wished rather to forget that he had ever been one of them. They were nothing but hyenas preparing to fight over the bones the lions left after the feast.

It was with a feeling of relief that he regained Ai-gams, and soon in the growing excitement there he was able to forget the unpleasant encounter. Time after time bands of raiders went out and Garib waited to be called to accompany them for now that he had seen the shame of his family, he wished more than ever to prove his own worth through manly deeds. No one knew where the expeditions were bound for, for Jonker Afrikaner kept his plans secret even from his leaders, but Kaptein Pieter told him, in answer to his impatient questions, that he had no need to feel envy. These were not glorious battles against great enemies. Only a few men were needed to start the rout with the sound of their guns and to round up the cattle afterwards. Maherero and his men were here to do all the fighting that was necessary. Was Jonker Afrikaner a fool to bark himself when he had dogs to do this for him? No, like a great cat, Haramub was merely sharpening his claws in preparation for the real battle.

Garib knew which battle Kaptein Pieter meant. It made no difference that Haramub had deliberately provoked the Cattle King. No man might attack Jonker Afrikaner and go unscathed. In increasing excitement and suspense Garib waited.

And though he took no part in the raids, Haramub did not forget those whom he left behind to guard his town when it was time to share out the captured cattle, and because Garib was ranked among the important men he received almost as many beasts as Kaptein Pieter himself. In wonder he watched his herds growing. He could never have earned as many through breaking in ride- or pack-oxen.

Then at last, at the end of the winter season, when the river beds lay like dry dusty roads in the valley and the hills were bare, a messenger came running to Garib's hut.

"You are to be ready at dawn to go with the Great Chief!"

Garib listened almost in disbelief. He had waited so long he had begun to think the day when he would be called would never come, and though, as usual, the purpose of the expedition was kept secret, he saw that many men about the town were cleaning their guns and preparing their ammunition. All the best and the most important men had been chosen to go. Ai-gams would be left virtually undefended. What could this raid be but the long-planned battle against Kahitjene himself?

Garib could sleep but little that night, and in the morning he joined the other men gathering outside the chief's hut. Some were on horses, some on ride oxen, shadowy figures in the pale grey light, their foodbags, waterbottles and blankets strapped to their saddles. They looked wild and gay with ostrich feathers waving from their hats and jackal tails flowing from the muzzles of their guns.

As they passed the white-washed buildings of the mission station Garib saw that the missionary who had rebuked the chief once before was standing, still and silent, beside the door. When the men saw him some of them shouted greetings.

"Pray for the success of our expedition, Man of God!" one of them called.

The missionary turned his head. "I shall not pray for such an evil," he said. "You and you and you!" He pointed to some of the men who had stopped to hear him. "You come to my church but you do not listen to my words."

"*Eisey*, master!" said one little man. "You are too hard on us. Tell us you are still our friend."

149

"Yes, yes!" cried several of the others, holding out their hands eagerly for they wished the Man of God to think well of them.

The missionary glanced at their outstretched hands, but made no move to take them. "I will not shake hands with wicked people," he said.

Garib, who had stopped also, saw the hurt on the men's faces, then, when the Man of God continued to ignore them, their sorrow turned quickly to anger.

"Why should you not shake our hands?" the little man said hotly. "And why should you not pray for our success? Our people have always prayed to Tsui-Goab before battle. What use is a god if he does not protect his people?"

"Yes, yes!" echoed some of the others, though Garib saw that several of the younger men seemed ill at ease and when the others began to ride away, they hesitated and kept looking back fearfully.

"Perhaps the missionary is right to condemn us," Garib heard one of them whisper. "Do not even the old people say that it is Gaunab, the Evil One, who is the maker of war? I do not wish for the flames of Hell." But his companion told him to come or he would miss his share of the prize, and in another moment they were all galloping off to catch up with Haramub.

Garib gazed after them. He did not know if it was the lack of sleep or the dryness of the air, but he suddenly felt heavy and drowsy. Our people are not good enough for the White Men's God, he thought. With an effort he lifted his head and was about to jerk the reins to follow the others when he saw that the missionary had come forward and was standing beside him.

"Why do you go with them?" the Man of God asked, looking up.

And suddenly Garib's heart began to pound and his throat tightened so that he could hardly breathe. The pale grey eyes of the missionary seemed to have such power that they held Garib and he could do nothing but look back into them.

"Why do you go against the Word of God?" the man demanded.

"I go because my chief tells me to go, master," Garib said

and to his own ears his voice had the foolish whine of a child. Would he never know his own strength as a man?

"Are you a dog to come when you are whistled for and to bark without asking why?" said the Man of God sternly. "If you are a dog, run after your master. But if you are a man, then think! A man knows what he must do. He knows that, while obeying the lawful commands of his chief, he must in the first place obey God."

Garib gazed down in helpless horror at the missionary. He felt he must surely drown in the steady depths of those grey eyes. But how could he stay when this was the day he had yearned for? How could he stay when he knew that on this day he might walk the road to glory? With a mighty effort he looked away. Already the last of the men on ride-oxen were disappearing into the thorn forest. Blind panic welled up in Garib.

"I cannot stay!" he shouted, hardly knowing what he was saying. "I have sent my kaross ahead on the pack-oxen and my chief waits for me." And with desperate haste he dug his heels into his horse's flanks and galloped away as if Gaunab himself were after him.

Eighteen

Towards evening Garib and the other horsemen reached Jonker Afrikaner's camp on the plain on the other side of the mountains. The white tent coverings of the wagons were hidden among the trees and Garib saw that men were converging on it from all directions and he knew that this raid was indeed to be a big one. Not only soldiers of the Warlike People and their servants were to take part, but men from the Nama tribes also, and everywhere people were walking about purposefully and the atmosphere was so tense with excitement that Garib could almost feel it, like a living thing, in the air.

He saw with surprise that Fast Foot was there too, standing beside his ride-ox with his big bow slung over his arm. But when he gave the matter thought, Garib knew that if he were a chief planning an important battle he too would have chosen his old friend as one of the men. Slow in thought Fast Foot might be, and now almost middle-aged, but he was a man to be relied on beyond all others, and, though he owned no gun, he was still as fast as a buck when he ran and could bend the bow with all the skill of a master hunter.

Garib was filled with warmth towards Fast Foot. It had been wrong of him to allow the friendship to lapse. Whom among his new acquaintances could he trust as he had trusted this man?

Quickly Garib tethered his horse to a tree near one of the wagons. He meant to go over to Fast Foot, but as he walked into the camp Kaptein Pieter called to him to come and give his opinion as to the destination of the expedition. And soon the honey beer was being passed around and Garib forgot all about the hunter. He was caught up again in the general excitement as the men argued and laughed and boasted and told stories of great deeds of bravery as men always did before battle.

For most of the night they kept up the carousing and hardly had silence fallen on the camp than the Kapteins were moving about shaking the men, for it was dawn.

Still half-drugged with beer and sleep, the men gathered into groups, all looking expectantly towards Jonker Afrikaner's wagon, and in a short while the little chief came out. In the pale light he looked small and portly in his White Man's coat and waistcoat and moleskin trousers, but his movements were still quick and supple and his eyes, which had narrowed with age and long exposure to bright sunshine, were alert, and Garib saw with relief that he was sober.

"Men of the Men of Men! Men of the Superior People!" The early morning air was crisp and fresh and at the sound of their chief's voice the men began to rouse themselves from their apathy. "Yes, my chief! *A, khub!*" came murmurs and shouts from all around.

Jonker Afrikaner held up his hand. "Today we ride to Okahandja, the home of Kahitjene!"

There was a great cheer and Garib's hand tightened on the butt of his gun till his knuckles showed white with pressure. It was as everyone had thought. Today was to be the day of the great battle. Now at last, after so many seasons of waiting, he, Garib Arub, was to test his strength against the enemy he had sworn to kill.

"And today," cried Jonker Afrikaner, "we shall all be rich beyond our wildest imaginings for it is on these plains where Kahitjene's main villages lie and where most of his great herds are kept!"

Now the shouts and cheers were deafening and Garib, suddenly remembering the countless number of Kahitjene's cattle he had watched passing by Kamoja's house, knew that indeed there was a mighty prize to be won. This would be a battle any man would wish to fight.

Once again Jonker Afrikaner raised his hand and the clamour ceased. "Today we shall destroy these dogs who dared to insult us! But listen to me!" he shouted. "Tjamuaha, who is my friend, also has villages on this plain, and though Tjamuaha is also a dog, he is my servant and his son Maherero and his men are of use to me when there is work to be done which does not befit a man. So leave my friend's villages and leave his cattle, and leave also the White Men who recently built a mission station at Okahandja so that they might teach the Cattle People, for I have no wish for trouble with the Governor at the Cape. So leave these," he cried, "but destroy all others!"

Quickly then the men with their guns in their hands and their bullet pouches strapped around them, mounted and set off across the plain. Riding close behind the leaders, Garib felt his skin tingling as the cold air beat against it. Eagerly he jerked the reins to urge his horse to go faster, then, in an agony of impatience, had to hold him back for he must not outstrip the leaders. Never had he been so excited. His elation made him remember the hunting trips he had made with Fast Foot on mornings just like this. But this was far more exciting than hunting animals. When one hunted the buck or even the lion one pursued it with stealth and cunning, but also with indifference for it was only a beast. But when people hunted other men, whom they hated and from whom they wished to take a great prize, they faced an enemy equal to themselves in cleverness, opponents against whom they must use the whole of their courage, and their lust for revenge and their greed were far more intoxicating than any brandy.

As the first light appeared in the sky the long line of soldiers met the spies which had been sent out to scout the way. In silence the men obeyed the hushed order of their kapteins. Keeping close to the edge of the range of hills, they moved nearer to Okahandja.

By the time the sky was grey several of Kahitjene's villages had come into sight, slender columns of smoke rising from some of the mud roofs. With no sound except that made by the hooves of the horses and oxen the men took up their positions, the horsemen and ox-riders in the centre and the unmounted men with other horsemen on each flank.

Slowly the horsemen in the centre moved forward down the slope and those on the flanks spread out into an arc to encircle the group of huts.

And suddenly, like a harsh tearing of cloth, the stillness of the morning was broken. The dogs behind the thorn fences began to bark wildly and Kaptein Pieter gave the signal to attack. At once the whole face of the hill became one great vivid streak of fire as a hailstorm of bullets rained down on to the unsuspecting houses. The crash of the reports echoed and re-echoed against the rocks, and the volumes of smoke that came from the guns and rifles were so dense that the whole scene below was hidden from the view of the advancing army.

Then as the smoke cleared Garib saw that the villages had come to sudden life. People were running in all directions and women and children were screaming with fright.

"It is the Men of Men! It is the Men of Men!"

Garib rammed another bullet into his gun with hands trembling with haste for he thought that the Cattle People meant to rush upon them as Kamoja's warriors had rushed upon the Big One, but as he raised his weapon his hands paused in mid air. The men were not coming towards them. They were running as fast as they could to find shelter behind the rocks and bushes of the plain. Many of them were not even carrying their spears, but, snatching up their children, were running crouching through the undergrowth.

Keeping his seat on his frightened horse with difficulty, Garib saw how it was. These men of Kahitjene, having experienced the terror of Jonker Afrikaner's guns once before when they had made the attack on the Warlike People, knew how futile it was to stand against them. But what they did not seem yet to know was that horses were able to move much faster than people.

"They are running!" screamed Hendrick close to Garib, and with shrieks and yells Jonker Afrikaner's horsemen were after the fleeing Black Men. And as they thundered down on the helpless people below, every bush and rock and hollow seemed to come alive with dark leaping, running bodies as the Cattle People left their places of hiding and ran in terror towards the nearby thickets of thorn trees. As they ran they leapt and screamed and fell as a fresh hail of bullets tore through them so that the ground was soon covered with the dead and bodies lay in mounds like anthills everywhere among the scrub.

Garib saw then that he had been wrong. This was not to be a great battle of courage between men of equal strength. This was to be a massacre.

From village to village the horsemen galloped. The Cattle People had no chance against the guns. Everywhere they were running and falling, too weighted down by their heavy strings of iron beads to escape, and, frenzied by the terrible sound of gunfire, the oxen had also broken from their pens and were charging about wildly, adding to the confusion.

And now the plundering began. Loud shouts and cries of exultation rang across the plain as the men loaded their horses and oxen with pots and calabashes, and decked themselves out in the iron ornaments and copper bangles torn from the dead, and the raiders, finding pots of honey beer in some of the huts, were soon shrieking with mirth as they stumbled about among the corpses. Garib felt dizzy with shock when he realized that all this was nothing new to Jonker Afrikaner's men.

Then a laughing voice nearby shouted, "David! David! Is your stomach as weak as that of a woman to be turned by the sight of blood, Lion-killer?" It was Kaptein Pieter and he was grinning across at Garib from the back of his big black horse. "If you take no part in the plundering you will go home a poor man. Here, catch!" he cried, throwing Garib a string of heavy beads from the many hanging from his arms.

As Garib caught the heavy coil blood spattered from it on to his shirt. Men said that the blood of one's enemies could make a man strong. Garib stared down at it, suppressing a shudder. He knew by now that Jonker Afrikaner's kind of warfare was not the same as that which had been praised in song by men like his father, Arub the Hunter, and that, though Haramub's soldiers might boast with swelling words as any other men before battle, when the fight was over there must be many things of which they could not boast at all. But if the way to greatness lay along this road Garib knew that he must take it for he had come too far with Haramub to turn back now. He hung the dripping string of beads on his saddle and forced himself to smile back at Kaptein Pieter.

"That is better, David," said the Kaptein, his eyes still gleaming with friendly mockery. "And now you must come with me for this is the chief's order. Kahitjene is trying to escape. He was warned by the sound of our guns early this morning and was leaving Okahandja with his cattle and a large number of his people when the right flank of our horsemen caught up with him. Many of those with him were killed and all the cattle fell into our hands, but Kahitjene himself and about twenty of his men got away from us and fled to the White Men's mission for protection. They are hiding in the church. Some of our men are there now, guarding the building, and we must go to them so that Kahitjene may be captured."

Garib and Kaptein Pieter galloped at speed through the tall trees that grew on the other side of the wide flat river bed. It was not far to the church. In a short while they reached the small wooden building. Close to it was the mission house, constructed of clay and neatly thatched with reeds. A crowd of Jonker Afrikaner's men were standing in front of it and as Garib came closer he saw that the walls of both the church and the mission house were battered with musket balls.

Then he saw with surprise that Fast Foot was there too. There was an astonished expression on his face as if he too had found the massacre like some awful dream and had sought refuge from it with the men waiting at the mission.

But there was no time to worry about Fast Foot now for Kaptein Pieter was speaking. "The chief will not allow us to storm the church," the Kaptein said as the men gathered round to receive instructions. "He says we are to use a trick instead to flush this rat from his hole." He grinned. "Wait, I will show you."

Kaptein Pieter walked up to the church door. "Kahitjene!" he shouted. "You think you are safe in there, but I tell you you will not be safe for long. We are going away now but we will be back shortly with burning brands. The thatch roof of the church will burn like dry grass, Kahitjene! Come out now and give yourself up or it will be the worse for you!"

There was silence from within the building and after a few moments Kaptein Pieter turned and walked back to his men. "Come," he said quietly. "Mount your horses and make a great show of leaving, but as soon as you are out of sight behind those bushes, stop. Only a madman or a fool would stay in a house which he knew was to be burnt and Kahitjene is neither. So keep your guns ready for you will have use for them."

"Fast Foot!" hissed Garib, suddenly feeling exasperation towards this slow man who continued to stand as if in a dream. Fast Foot stared at him blankly, then followed obediently.

As soon as the men were hidden behind the bushes they stopped and some of them dismounted and took up positions in the thicket from where they could cover the entrance to the church.

Fast Foot came up behind Garib's horse. "Young One," he whispered, but Garib motioned him to silence impatiently. Why did Fast Foot persist in calling him by this name even though he had long since left childhood behind?

They waited for what seemed a long time.

"He is not going to fall for your ruse, my Kaptein," said one of the men softly.

"Look!" cried another, leaping up. "Look! Kahitjene was indeed no fool. See, there he is! He came out through some back way and is already escaping!"

With shouts of rage the men left their cover to give chase, and at once an arrow hissed through the air and a man fell with the feathered shaft still quivering in his throat and another arrow twanged into a nearby tree trunk.

"*Eisey!*" shouted someone. "Be careful! They are hiding behind those rocks to the side of the church!"

"Get them!" screamed Kaptein Pieter and Garib jerked his horse forward. The horse reared up on its hind legs in fright as yet another arrow whirred past it.

"Come back! You will be killed, David!" shouted one of the men behind him. "Guns cannot shoot through rock and the arrows are poisoned!"

But Garib hardly heard him for suddenly he could bear no more of the cowardly massacre. The thought of the slaughter which he knew was still going on all around was like a madness in his head, and the words, "Young One, Young One, Young One", kept echoing through his brain as if taunting him to prove his manhood once and for all.

He was aware that he was the only man obeying the Kaptein's order, but he did not care. In his desperate need to make this battle the thing of glory he had hoped it would be, he brought his switch down on the horse's flank with a stinging blow. The horse snorted again and plunged forward.

An arrow shot past Garib's ear, and another and another, and from behind came the sound of rifle fire, and the bullets struck against the rocks in a shower of sparks. The men behind the boulders left their place of shelter in panic and began to run wildly towards the bushes. Garib saw Kahitjene among them and whipped his horse again to pursue him.

"Wait, Garib!" shouted a voice behind him, and in a moment there was a man running with incredible speed beside him.

"Fast Foot!"

The look of bewilderment was gone from Garib's friend's face. He had shed his sandals and dropped his bow. Instead in his hand was his hunting knife and in his eyes was the keen triumphant expression Garib had seen so often when the hunter had been about to overtake a herd of zebra. At last something was happening which Fast Foot could understand.

"I am with you, Garib!" he panted.

Every moment they were gaining on the fleeing Cattle People. Then one of the Black Men turned. It was Kahitjene himself. And, as if seeing that flight was useless, he stopped to face his pursuers and raised his bow. The next instant the bow string twanged. Garib jerked his horse to the side and heard the poisoned dart singing past. Kahitjene had missed him! He gave a wild exultant cry. This was how battle should be, man pitting his strength against man with courage. There was a strange strangled sound beside him. Still with his blood racing joyfully through his veins, Garib turned and looked down and the wild cry died on his lips. Below him on the ground Fast Foot was doing a strange dance, hands clutched at his throat, and between his fingers, like some peculiar flower bursting from the dry earth, was the stiff feathered shaft of an arrow.

In a moment Garib was off his horse. He caught Fast Foot as he fell. "Fast Foot! Fast Foot, my friend!" he cried. But Fast Foot was already dead.

For a long season of time Garib knelt with the hunter in his arms. He gazed with shock that was like a tearing pain into the open staring eyes. "Fast Foot!" he whispered. Ever since Garib could remember the master hunter with the thin knotted legs had been a part of his life. For some time now, impatient with his slowness, Garib had taken little notice of him, but now suddenly he knew what a great debt he owed this man. Fast Foot had taught him to hunt and it was Fast Foot who had stayed behind in the battle against Kamoja to try to save him. And with terrible anguish he remembered also how his friend had stayed with him, sleepless with anxiety, on the night before his fight with the lion, and had nursed his wounds with more gentleness than he had known even from his own mother. And it was Fast Foot among all the other men who had rushed out to help him pursue Kahitjene. And now Fast Foot was dead, and it was Kahitjene who had killed him.

As if repeating a verse from the wisdom the missionaries had tried to teach him, Garib whispered, "Kahitjene killed my father, and it was Kahitjene too who killed Fast Foot."

Slowly he let the hunter's body sink on to the earth. He stood up. He looked towards where Kahitjene had been standing.

"Where is he?" he asked Kaptein Pieter who had come up behind him.

"He has escaped with his men into the forest," said the Kaptein. "We cannot follow in that thick bush."

Garib clenched his fists. All his life he had known that one day he must kill Kahitjene, but as the seasons had passed he had forgotten much of the pain and bitterness. Now hatred burst inside him. He turned to face the direction Kahitjene had gone.

"I will kill you, Kahitjene!" he screamed. "I will kill you."

There was low slurred laughter behind him. With eyes blazing in his pale face, Garib spun round, ready to lash out at anyone who came near. It was Jonker Afrikaner and Garib saw at once that he was no longer sober.

The little chief was sitting on his brown horse, grasping at the reins. He was so drunk that he could scarcely keep from falling. As he saw Garib's anger fade into surprise he laughed again. "Well spoken, my Slayer of Lions!" he said. "You wish to kill this Kahitjene and so you shall. Twice the dog has escaped me, but he shall not escape a third time. I shall hunt him till he stands helpless as a jackal against a cliff, and in this you shall help me, David, my David, and you shall be my Kaptein."

Nineteen

When Jonker Afrikaner and his people returned to Ai-gams after the massacre of Okahandja, they brought with them enormous herds of cattle, but their hatred of the Cattle People seemed greater than ever. They started to drive out all those families of Black Men who had left their own clans and come to live near Haramub during the time of peace. They attacked every unprotected village and, to show their anger at the hurtful rebukes of the Men of God, they piled the dead bodies near to the mission house.

Soon after that the missionaries packed up their wagons and left the valley of the Winterhoek.

"We can find no way to teach you and your people the Word of God," they told Haramub, "for you are nothing but a low cattle thief."

Jonker Afrikaner said nothing, but his eyes were as cold and hard as they had been when he had listened to Kahitjene's insult, and Garib thought that it was as well for the White Men that Haramub feared their Governor in the Cape. And as soon as they were gone he called for his brandy like a man who has pain which he cannot bear, and after that he was rarely sober, even in the mornings.

And then the raiding was able to go on without any pretence at all and the people no longer had to hide under their karosses in the darkness of their huts when the Men of God came to scold them. And though there was no game left to hunt anywhere near Ai-gams, the men of Haramub now hunted the Black Men as if they were wild animals. As the hunters had once waited for the zebra at the waterhole, building screens of bushes to hide them from view of their unwary prey, so

Jonker Afrikaner's soldiers now awaited the Cattle People at the pools, knowing that all men must come for water; as they had once ambushed the springbok wandering in herds, they now lay in wait behind boulders and hid in rocky retreats to fire upon the fleeing clans; and as, in the early days, men had stood in wide circles on the grassy plain to beat up the hares and knock them down with their clubs, so they now encircled helpless villages so that none might escape.

Before many moons had passed forty villages of the Cattle People had been destroyed and, as closely as men could count, eleven thousand cattle captured on the plains north of Ai-gams, and every day fugitives from the guns of the Warlike People fled in their despair to the missionaries and the White traders or made their homes fearfully in the bush.

Destitute of cattle and with no milk to drink or beef to eat, the Black People who survived wandered about the land like walking skeletons, living on roots and berries and following the vultures, and these men who had once been so arrogant fought like hyenas over the bones and scraps which the lions had left half eaten, and those who had once owned such great herds and been masters over such vast lands lived in poverty which equalled that of the most wretched Bushman.

Indeed Garib saw that it was as he had feared. All the Men of Men were proud and fierce, but Jonker Afrikaner had become cruel beyond even the fierceness of his nature and now, like a wild beast turned rogue in the festering pain of an unhealed hurt, was tearing to pieces all within his reach as if he wished to avenge himself on the whole world. Before in warfare the women and children had been spared and the vanquished had always been allowed to return to their homes and bury the dead. But Haramub's warfare was like nothing which had ever been seen before. Whole clans were slaughtered, every hut was burnt, and with no one left alive to bury the dead, the rotting bodies were left for the vultures and the jackals, and the wild beasts grew bold and fearless from feeding on human flesh.

And just as the Nama tribes had, because of tribal jealousies, been unable to unite to fight against the invading Cattle People in the time of the great drought, so now the Black

Men, though they were still far greater in numbers than the Men of Men, did not join together to overthrow their small masters for they could not cease from fighting against each other.

Vast stretches of grassland where once many villages had stood and where fine fat cattle had grazed in great herds, lay silent and empty under the sun, and the whole land trembled at the sound of Jonker Afrikaner's name and men fled in terror even from a whirlwind of dust, fearing it might be dust raised by the hooves of Haramub's horses.

Now indeed Haramub had fulfilled the great boast he had made on that day so long ago in the house of Arub the Big One when he was still a homeless wanderer and one of the scorned wearers of hats. The great lands to the north were his and so were the vast herds of the Black Men's cattle.

And though the chiefs of some of the Nama tribes in the south, who had taken missionaries and were trying to keep the Word of God, expressed displeasure at the cruelty with which Jonker Afrikaner was treating the Cattle People, the little chief paid no heed. He knew that no one could stand against him.

And the men of the Warlike People, taking their example from their chief, became arrogant beyond all others.

"Work?" they asked when their wives complained that there were no longer any crops of calabashes to be picked beside the hot springs. "Must we be like worms, then, and dig in the ground? What fools we would be to plant gourds when there are still gardens in the north where we may reap crops more to our liking than melons!"

And Tjamuaha too soon learnt what it was like to have a wounded leopard for a master for, though his cattle were still safe and growing in numbers, the price he had to pay for his safety was high. His men had to kill and plunder for Haramub and in return were treated worse than dogs by the Men of Men. Tjamuaha became know as "Jonker's Dog" and his son, Maherero, was constantly being tied to the wagon wheel for no other reason than that Haramub wished to show the people that he was indeed master of the land.

Garib saw all these things, but his own hatred of Kahitjene

was now so strong that it seemed he could think of nothing else. And as Jonker Afrikaner hunted the other Cattle People, he hunted Kahitjene also, but whereas he showed nothing but cold indifference to the fate of the others, he hounded the Cattle King with a ruthless vindictiveness as if he triumphed in destroying him. As Garib, now one of Haramub's kapteins, led his horsemen against the remaining scattered families belonging to this man who had once been the greatest and the richest chief among the Cattle People, sweeping away village after village until his wealth in men and cattle was almost gone, he could not help thinking that this was how the men of Arub had hunted game too big and too dangerous to be attacked openly. This was how, in the time of Garib's learning to be a hunter, they had fought with the fierce black rhinoceros, hurling spears first from one side, then from the other, allowing it no chance to rest until, unable to go further from wounds and exhaustion, the great beast had fallen helpless and groaning to the ground. And like the rhinoceros in its death throes, Kahitjene was rushing from place to place, trying to escape from Jonker Afrikaner and to save his people.

But though Garib's hatred for the Cattle King was as great as the little chief's, he was unable to feel triumph at Kahitjene's defeats, even though he received a kaptein's share of all the captured cattle so that he was fast becoming himself a rich man. While still a child he had discovered that strange thing that when one hurt another one might feel the wound in one's own body. Now he found that hatred too might reflect back on the one who hated, and he could feel no liking for himself or take any pride in his new position which gave him a greatness he had scarcely dared even to hope for.

But neither could he cease from his hating or turn from his purpose. He was like a man who had been staggering for many days across the dry plains without water and had now found the waterhole he longed for, but no matter how much he drank he was unable to quench his thirst, and the more he drank, the more his craving for water increased.

"I shall kill this Kahitjene," he vowed over and over. "I shall kill him for this is what I must do, and when blood has paid for blood I shall surely find peace."

Then towards the close of the rainy season, when the thorn trees were in full bloom, Jonker Afrikaner called for Garib. Garib found the little chief sitting hunched up in his hut wrapped in his skin kaross. He smiled when he saw Garib and held out a hand that trembled slightly.

"David," he said. "I see you so seldom. You are so busy now, my Kaptein David! So great! You no longer have time for an old man."

Garib knew then that Haramub was in one of his melancholy moods which so often came upon him after he had drunk too much of the White Men's brandy. His eyes were rheumy and red-rimmed and his face looked old. Often Garib felt that he hated Haramub for the shame he was forcing upon him, but now, looking at him, he felt a quick sharp pity for he saw that this great chief who was master of the whole country was worse than a slave to his own cravings.

"*Ai*, David!" Jonker Afrikaner said. "Sit. Sit for I have news for you which will make your heart glad."

Garib sat down beside the chief. A cold apprehension clutched at him.

"When you were only a boy, David, you ran to me and stopped my horse. You told me then that you wished to kill Kahitjene and now after more than twenty years this is still your wish. *Eisey!* David! Many men have dreams of glory but few are able to keep their eye on the road so that they achieve their goal. And when I saw you, even though you were a boy, I knew that you were like me and would not rest until you had done what you planned to do. So now I have news for you about Kahitjene."

The little chief paused. "As you know it is not only my soldiers who have been attacking the old Cattle King. Other clans of the Cattle People, seeing that his strength was gone, have fallen on him to make up their own losses and have taken even that which I left. Now Kahitjene has no cattle except a few thin beasts at his home in the north, and no warriors except forty starved men who will desert him like dogs at the first shot, and in his last battle against his uncle's people even his son was killed. Now he is indeed like a beast that stands helpless against a cliff. He is of no more use to me for all I wished for was his cattle, but you wished for his blood, so now I call you as I promised."

Jonker Afrikaner patted Garib's hand. "This son of Kahitjene's who was killed was buried not far from here over the mountains near his enemy's village. My spies tell me that the Cattle King means to view this son's grave as is the custom among the Cattle People. He knows that it will mean his life if he walks into the country of his enemy, but Kahitjene, though old and poor, has not learnt wisdom. He is still proud and foolish in his courage. My spies tell me he set out from his home yesterday for he believes, with his people, that his son's spirit cannot rest in peace until he has visited the place of his burial. On his way Kahitjene must go through the stony pass between the hills to the north. Tomorrow morning you will wait there for him, David, and you will kill him."

Twenty

Garib sat crouched behind a boulder on the side of the stony divide through which Kahitjene and his warriors were to pass. Higher up the kloof were three of Haramub's men, hidden behind other rocks, their guns at the ready. The plan was to ambush the impoverished Cattle King when he was well into the narrow defile and separate him from his men who would be following him so that he would fall an easy prey to Garib who waited lower down. It was a plan which could not fail for, though Kahitjene was reported to have forty men escorting him and the Men of Men numbered only four, bowmen caught unprepared could not hope to stand against gunmen who fired from the safety of a rocky hillside, and, as Jonker Afrikaner knew full well, all Cattle People were filled with terror by the sound of rifle fire.

Garib wiped his forehead on his sleeve and replaced his dark hat. The sun was too hot. His eyes were narrowed almost to slits in the glare which reflected from the large pale stones and the heat in the divide was oppressive. He moved his gun slightly so that it rested more firmly in a niche in the boulder in front of him and set his sights for the opening between the two rocks which jutted out from the banks on either side. When Kahitjene ran for cover he would have to pass between those two rocks and would come face to face with Garib. The day Garib had waited for for so long had come at last.

Suddenly a baboon barked higher up the kloof. It was so well done that Garib wondered if it might perhaps be a real baboon. The bark came three times. It was the signal from the first of Haramub's men that Kahitjene had entered the pass.

Garib sat without moving, staring at the opening between the boulders. Heat waves danced on the surface of the rock. He licked his lips but his mouth felt dry and parched. He waited.

At first he could hear nothing, then faintly came the shouts of Kahitjene's men as they called to each other cheerfully. Garib could see it all in his mind's eye. Kahitjene would be leading the way, his heavy clubs in his waistband, his bow over his arm and his spear in his right hand, and behind him, after the manner of the Cattle People, would come the long line of men in single file.

The shouts came nearer, resounding against the rocks as the unsuspecting men advanced into the trap.

Then the first shot came. It ripped and tore through the still hot air, a terrible shocking sound. Even when it had faded away it seemed to go on ringing in Garib's head and the sounds which came after it seemed only echoes. There were more shots, then screams, and the loud knocking noise of stones, dislodged by the feet of the warriors fleeing up the hillside, bumping down on to the other stones below.

Then suddenly Kahitjene was standing in the opening between the boulders. His iron beads clattered as he pulled himself out of range of Jonker Afrikaner's men to what he imagined would be safety behind the rock nearest to Garib. His back was towards Garib, not more than four paces away, naked and exposed, a perfect target for a swift bullet. As if bound by some magic spell, Garib watched the dark, gleaming back rising and falling from the exertion of running. He watched Kahitjene lay down his spear so that he could reach for his bow and quiver of poisoned arrows.

Quickly Garib brought up his gun. It made a scraping sound on the rock. Kahitjene spun round, his hands empty of weapons and stood quite still with shock.

"Shoot!" shouted a voice inside Garib's head. "Shoot Kahitjene who killed your father and Fast Foot! Shoot the enemy of your people!"

Garib took aim. His finger trembled on the trigger, but still Kahitjene did not move. Slowly Garib's gaze rose from the Cattle King's chest and found his face. He saw lines of age and suffering deeply scored on either side of the mouth, but the eyes were still as bright and piercing as he remembered, and they were looking at him steadily.

"I see I have come to the end of my road," said Kahitjene breathlessly. "I can run no further, man of Haramub. So shoot. Why do you delay? Shoot me now that I face you and not in my back so that when my people find me they can know that I died like a man."

Garib tried to speak, but there was nothing to say. His hands were cold and damp so that they could scarcely grip the gun. "Shoot!" urged the voice in his head. "You have killed many other men. Kill this enemy also."

Desperately Garib tried to remember all the evil which Kahitjene had done to him and his people so that he might be filled again with hatred, but when he looked at the tall Cattle King standing before him, he saw only a man who was old, a man who had been hunted mercilessly like an animal, all his wealth stripped from him, until he stood now too exhausted to run further. And then Garib saw something more. As he gazed at Kahitjene he saw that the Black Man stood erect, his head well back, his eye unflinching as he waited for Garib to shoot, and he knew that the Cattle King, though old and impoverished and hunted, was still a man noble in courage.

Slowly Garib lowered his gun. For a long while the two men stared at each other, then, strangely, Kahitjene's gaze softened as if he had pity for Garib.

"My son," he said gently. "It is not easy to kill a man, but listen. When I set out on this journey I knew that I must die. My enemies among the Cattle People lie in wait for me at my son's grave. If you do not kill me as Haramub has ordered you, my uncle's people shall do this and more."

The tall Black Man stood as if expecting Garib to raise his gun once more, but Garib only continued to stare at him. For more than twenty years he had waited for this moment and now that it had come he knew that he could not kill Kahitjene.

"Go," he whispered. "But do not go on down the pass for there your enemies are waiting. Go back over the hill to your home while there is yet time."

Kahitjene gazed at him a moment longer, then slowly he

stooped and picked up his spear. "Your face is familiar to me," he said. "Were you not the messenger Haramub sent to me to ask for peace many seasons ago?"

Garib nodded. "I am Garib Arub," he said.

"Arub? Arub?" Kahitjene repeated the word thoughtfully as if trying to recall if he had ever heard of it. "No, I do not know your people," he said and Garib thought how strange it was that this man whose herdsmen had killed his father and forced his people southward through the terrible land of thirst so that he must always be their enemy, should not even know the name of Arub.

Then Kahitjene raised his hand as if even now he remembered his manners as a great chief. "Now I salute you, Garib Arub," he said, "but I cannot go back as you bid me. I must go on, for as my son's father and his chief it is my duty to see his grave." And turning, he walked on down the path which he knew led to his certain death.

And Garib, watching him go in anguish, thought that though this Kahitjene had, in the time of his power, been little better than Jonker Afrikaner in his plundering and cattle raiding, he was also a great man. He remembered what Tomarib had told him when trying to teach him wisdom. "A man must choose to act as a man and not as a beast." The old counsellor had taught him the words so well he could still remember it all. "I must not sit at a fire with people who have stolen cattle. I must not kill without cause. I must not lie." And there were all those other commandments the Men of God had made him learn. Garib knew then that they were true. Just as a man should not be killed like a beast, he should not live like one either.

And thinking of the terrible things which he and the other Men of Men had done in their greed and hatred, he put his head down on the butt of his gun and wept soundlessly.

When Garib returned to Ai-gams he did not know how to explain to Haramub that he had not been able to kill Kahitjene.

"He escaped from me," was all he said, and he listened as Jonker Afrikaner told him of how the old warrior had gone on into his enemy's territory and had been surrounded by his uncle's men and shot with an arrow, then stabbed to death with a single thrust of the spear near to the grave of his son. Kahitjene, the man whom it seemed Garib had hated all his life, was dead, but Garib could feel no exultation, only a kind of deadness as if he himself had been killed.

Haramub looked at him curiously as if he guessed at some part of his young kaptein's trouble, but Garib did not wish to speak of it to anyone. He wandered listlessly about the town and on the second day he went down to the old part of Ai-gams where the stone church Haramub had built still stood. It had not been used for many seasons and was falling into disrepair. Some of its windows were boarded up and its heavy wooden door hung drunkenly on broken hinges. Though he did not know why, Garib pushed open the door and went in.

It was dim inside the church and there was dust everywhere. Old packing cases were piled up in the front all round the pulpit and empty brandy bottles lay strewn on the floor between the wooden benches. Garib stood within the doorway staring about him, remembering the bright silks and satins and gay headdresses which had once made the scene so splendid. But it was very quiet in the church, all sound from the town shut out. The silence seemed to reach out to Garib like a restful hand.

Picking his way between the litter, he sat down on one of the benches. Before he had always felt uneasiness that was like a kind of fear when in the church, but he felt no fear now. There was nothing left to be afraid of in a place so destroyed. He bowed his head and closed his eyes as the missionaries had taught him to do. But to whom should he pray? To Tsui-Goab or to the White Man's God? Confused and finding no meaning in anything, he did not pray at all.

He just sat and after a while a drowsiness came over him and he seemed to hear singing and the distant drone of voices as if some echo of the words which had once been spoken in the broken church remained, even though all else was gone. He thought he heard children's voices reciting psalms and the deep solemn tones of the first Man of God who had stood in the pulpit, and the poetry of the verse came back to him.

"The wolf shall dwell with the lamb, and the leopard shall lie down with the kid; and the calf and the young lion and the fatling together and a little child shall lead them. They shall not hurt nor destroy in all my holy mountain for the earth shall be full of the knowledge of the Lord, as the waters cover the sea."

And once again Garib was amazed. The wolf and the lamb, the leopard and the baby goat? He knew that it was very good when peoples of different nations came together, but could such a thing ever come to be? Had the peace between the Men of Men and the Cattle People not been consumed again into the fires of hatred and greed? Were not men of different nations destined to be enemies forever? Garib did not know.

All he knew was that he was a rich man, great in the eyes of men. Was this not what the old soothsayer had promised him? Now it was his and he saw that there was no glory in this kind of greatness.

And in his despair he bent his head once more and whispered a kind of prayer.

"O God," he said, not caring to whom he was speaking. "Must a man travel for ever and still arrive at no place!"

Twenty-one

Garib no longer wished to stay in Ai-gams and began to think more and more of his mother and the sister he had not seen for so long, but he found it had been easier to join Haramub than it was to leave him. He was like a sheep which had walked easily and unsuspectingly into a hakisthorn bush to graze on the leaves, and, now that he wanted to move away, found that the thorns were long and curved inward so that the more he struggled to be free, the more entangled he became in the thicket. All Garib's wealth and position were tied up with Jonker Afrikaner, and the great herds which he had gained were cared for with Haramub's own beasts by Tjamuaha, his ally and servant, in the distant valleys. He would lose all if he tried to leave Haramub now and earn also the terrible revenge he knew must follow upon such an insult to the chief. And it seemed there was something else too which held him. Though he still felt hatred and horror when he thought of the things which Haramub made his people do, his pity for the little chief grew. The more Haramub ripped and tore like a wounded beast, the more he drank the brandy. Often he called for Garib when the melancholy which followed a great bout of drinking was upon him, and held his hand, and sometimes even wept, and Garib knew that he could not now leave this man who had given him his greatness. He must go on with him to the very end.

Soon the vast droves which had been captured were almost spent and more raids had to be made so that the traders might be paid, and soon everyone in the land knew that when the traders' wagons appeared over the hills it was the signal for the men of the Warlike People to begin to clean their guns so

174

that they might go and harvest their crops in the north.

But no matter how many cattle were captured there never seemed to be enough. Haramub's men spent their wealth lavishly when they had it and gave no thought to the morrow. And when they had no more cattle left to barter they became as importunate as beggars so that the traders began to pass by Ai-gams as quickly as possible for the people wished for everything and were unable to pay, and most of them were drunk all day on honey beer and lay like dogs in the grass with their faces turned upwards towards the sun. Looking about him, Garib could only find one thought to comfort himself and that was that Fast Foot had not lived to experience such degradation.

Soon Ai-gams was like a village which had been overrun by wild dogs. It was so dirty it was no longer a place where men might wish to live, and Jonker Afrikaner, as if he had forgotten his great hopes for his town with everything else he wished to forget in the brandy, left the valley of the Winterhoek and went to live at Okahandja near to the one who was his friend. He built a fort of stone and his people built their huts all around it on one side of the wide flat river, and Tjamuaha lived on the other side, and the friendship between the chiefs continued.

From his hut near to the fort Garib could see Tjamuaha's villages. He saw the thousands of Tjamuaha's cattle crowded on the slopes of the hills behind, and in the evenings he watched the tall Black Men busy about their many bright fires as they prepared the wild roots and bulbs for their meal. But Garib saw also that this friendship which enabled Tjamuaha to live when all others had been killed and to keep his cattle safe even within arm's reach of the terrible Haramub, was nothing but a partnership of hatred and greed, and the one whose shrewdness and cunning had made him the greatest and richest chief among the Cattle People, was nothing but a mouse caught between the claws of a cat. He dared not disobey his watching friend in anything.

Not only did Tjamuaha's people have to care for Haramub's herds as his servants, but when a raid was to be made it was Tjamuaha's son, Maherero, who had to attack and carry it through, even though the people he fought against were his own starving kinsmen.

And when Garib, as one of the kapteins, had to bring in the cattle of these people, his shame became unbearable. He remembered the vultures as he had seen them circling far above him when he had lain weak with thirst upon the great plain as a child, and he saw that he and Haramub's men were worse even than Arub the Big One and his band. They had been like hyenas, but the Warlike People were like vultures gathering about the helpless and dying body of the Cattle People.

When there were no more cattle to be found in the whole of the country of the Cattle People, Jonker Afrikaner took his wagons and went even further north to the land of the Ovambo tribes, leaving Garib with some of the men to guard his fort in Okahandja. When he returned he brought back with him twenty thousand head of cattle, but now even this was not enough. The beasts had hardly arrived at Okahandja than a strange disease brought from the north broke out among them and most of them died and the illness spread to some of the healthy cattle. Everywhere beasts were dying and then it seemed the end was coming so quickly that it swept all before it like a flood at the time of the storms.

And then suddenly Jonker Afrikaner was dying too. In consternation the people listened to the news. He too had brought back this evil from the land of the Ovambo and his body, so wasted already by his continuous drinking of the White Men's brandy, could not withstand the fever.

But, as if even now when Jonker Afrikaner was too weak to leave his bed, Tjamuaha still could not find the strength to disobey him, the chief of the Cattle People fell ill also. Tjamuaha lay in his hut on the north side of the Okahandja River and, not more than a hundred paces away, Jonker Afrikaner lay in his hut on the west side, and in fear and superstition the people watched for they saw that Haramub, as a final proof of his power, was determined that, if he must die, the one who was called his dog must die first.

The days passed and still the two men lived on. But Jonker

Afrikaner did not have the tall strong body of the Cattle Chief. He lay small and old and ill, almost lost among his soft sheepskin blankets, and his strength ebbed fast.

"Master David!" A servant came rushing to Garib's hut at dawn. "Come quickly!"

Numbed with apprehension, Garib dressed in haste and followed the servant. He found Haramub's son, Christian, and Maherero already beside the chief's bed.

"My David!" whispered Haramub. "Come closer."

Garib bent to catch his words.

"When I am dead you as my Kaptein must give Maherero all my clothes and my pipe, my stick and my old gun and also my cartridge belt for he has earned these."

With an effort he struggled into a sitting position and while two servants held him he picked up the shoe from his right foot and gave it to Christian and gave his left shoe to Maherero. "So it shall be," he panted. "My son has my right shoe and he must be first in the land, but Maherero has my left shoe and together they make a pair. They must stay side by side like brothers and live in peace."

Then as if he had no strength to fight any more, he lay back in his blankets and closed his eyes.

"Go now," he whispered, and Garib and the others crept out of the hut.

Three days later Jonker Afrikaner was dead.

When Tjamuaha heard that his tormentor was gone he too called for Maherero and Christian and the chief people of both nations. When all the men he had sent for had arrived Tjamuaha sat up without aid and beckoned to his son who for so long had had to bear the punishment of his friendship.

"My child," he said, "my people tell me that my friend who is now dead gave you his clothes and all the things of his personal use. So now I tell you to give all my possessions to Christian. And I am told also that my dead friend gave each of you one of his shoes to remind you that you are brothers. I shall do likewise."

He bent down and took off his sandals and gave them to Christian and Maherero and the people waited in silence.

"In my life I have not done much to help my people," he said to Maherero. "But this I promise you. When I am dead I shall close only one eye. With the other I shall watch over you from the land of the spirits."

The important men of both nations listened in awe for they had a great belief in the power of the words of a dying man, and they glanced at each other apprehensively for all had seen that Tjamuaha had not given his right shoe to Christian to show that he agreed that the son of Jonker Afrikaner should continue to be first in the land. Now that his watching friend was dead Tjamuaha had refused to agree, and had given it to his own son, Maherero. And Tjamuaha, seeing the glances, smiled shrewdly and secretly, and lying down again turned from them all to face the wall and in a short while he too was dead.

And suddenly in the afternoon there was a sound like thunder in the distance. A loud gust of wind came tearing through the trees, lifting up the dead leaves and sticks and dust. Like a great cloud, it was billowing and swirling across the plain. It rushed past the hut where Tjamuaha lay dead and turned southward towards the camp of the Men of Men.

Before they could escape out of its way, the whirlwind was upon Garib and those with him. It filled their eyes and noses with dust and tore the mats from the huts and carried them towards the south.

"It is Gaunab!" cried some of the men for it was believed that the Evil One might appear in a rush of wind. But the others stared after the whirling cloud in fear. "It is Tjamuaha's spirit coming as he promised and already he is pushing the Men of Men back towards the south!"

And Garib, looking up quickly, saw Maherero standing nearby and he saw a change come into the face of the one who had so often been tied like a dog to Haramub's wagon wheel, and he knew that the end had come.

Twenty-two

Just as the peace, which the missionaries had brought about between the Men of Men and the Cattle People, had lain like a fallen flower upon the ground for some while before it had been trampled into the dust, so now the mockery of friendship made between Jonker Afrikaner and Tjamuaha in fear and greed and, at their death, passed on to their sons, Christian and Maherero, continued even though open hatred was shown more clearly by both nations every day.

And as the hatred grew so the fear increased among the little Men of Men. They had always been afraid of the tall Black Men. Even when they had reduced them to the lowest kind of slavery so that they could scarcely be called human, they had still watched them with fearful suspicion. But before, when they had been alarmed they had always been able to say, "Haramub is with us. Haramub knows how to handle the Cattle People." Now Haramub was no more, and without the little chief to direct them with energy and cleverness, they were like a body without a head. They sat outside their huts in the sun and drank honey beer and spoke great boasting words, and, like people who lived in a dream, they watched the clouds of trouble gathering and did nothing.

With scorn for the elaborate ceremonies of the Cattle People, they watched Maherero and his people go through their sacred duties following Tjamuaha's death. The body of the old chief, wrapped in hides, was buried at the entrance to his cattle enclosure and when the grave was filled in with earth, the great branch of a tree was placed at the head of it, and on it were hung Tjamuaha's bow and quiver and his fine war dress. Amid great weeping, the slaughtering of the sacred oxen began and each day the number of horns thrown upon the grave increased until they made a huge pile of bleaching bones, and every afternoon the wailing started and continued far into the night, and the Men of Men, listening to the deep throbbing sound of it, became more scornful than ever to hide their fear.

Then Maherero made a new sacred fire with his own kindling sticks as was the custom for a new chief, and then all the people who were kinsmen of Tjamuaha left their places of hiding, and many even came down from the north, so that they too might view the dead chief's grave as was fitting.

The Men of Men watched the numbers of Cattle People who were streaming into Okahandja from all sides in growing dismay. They had not known that so many Black Men still existed. Only a few seasons ago the nation of the Cattle People had lain as if dying while the vultures gathered. Now the change which Garib had seen in Maherero's face was beginning to show in them too. Everywhere the Cattle People were stirring. Life was coming back into them. They walked with a new step and carried their heads high as they had used to do before their subjection, and reports kept arriving at Christian Afrikaner's fort that slaves were even beginning to resist their masters and some of those who had been cattle herdsmen were disappearing in the night, taking with them all the cattle and sheep of which they had been in charge.

Anxiously the Men of Men began to think of their flocks of sheep and their herds of cattle which had escaped the sickness and were in the care of Maherero's people.

"Why do you not send me the possessions Tjamuaha promised me at his death?" asked Christian. "Is this how you show your friendship?" And back came the answer, "It is not the custom among the Cattle People to divide the inheritance until the year of mourning is over and all the kinsmen have viewed the grave."

These words gave the Men of Men no reassurance and some of those who knew that the Cattle People would never give over things which had been worn on a chief's person to an enemy lest they work evil magic with them, began to think also of the many guns which Maherero had received from

Jonker Afrikaner or bought himself from the traders. But still they did nothing. They went on sitting in the sun and drinking honey beer and at last the year of mourning came to an end.

"What will happen now?" Garib asked Kaptein Pieter as he stood with him outside the fort.

Kaptein Pieter wiped his dusty face on his sleeve. "Maherero and his people will move their village to a new place for this is their custom." He grinned but there was no mirth in his smile. "They fear the vengeance of a dead chief's spirit if they stay at the place where he died."

"Where will they go?"

Kaptein Pieter shrugged. "Maherero tells Christian nothing."

It was obvious to Garib that Kaptein Pieter knew no more than he did, but still he lingered for there was nothing else to do. Once more the summer was upon them and the heat was oppressive. Garib leant against the wall of the fort and rested his gun on the ground and after a while, to pass the time, Kaptein Pieter began to talk of other matters.

"A trader came yesterday," he said. "His wagons are lower down the river. He will not come any closer to Okahandja for he says that the people try to steal his brandy. They say he sits with his rifle on his knees while the people trade."

Both men laughed at this thought, then Kaptein Pieter yawned and said, "They say he is waiting here until he finds drovers to help him herd his bartered cattle down to the Great River." And they laughed again for they knew how lazy all the people had become. There were no better herdsmen than the quick little Men of Men, but they preferred to lie in the sun.

"Where is he going?" asked Garib, brushing away a persistent fly.

"First Ai-gams, then Hoachanas in the south where the missionaries have made a station among Oasib's people." He paused. "Hoachanas. Is that not where you told me your people were, David?"

Garib looked away. "Yes," he said. "The family of Arub has now broken up, but my mother lives there with my sister."

181

"And you have never been back to visit them, David?" asked the Kaptein, pretending to be amazed. "*Ai*, Lion-killer! I am glad you are not my son!"

Cut to the quick, Garib answered, "How can I leave Okahandja? My work has always been with Haramub. And I must be a fool to leave my herds of cattle now when they are in Maherero's care!" And, picking up his gun, he walked angrily away and tried to close his ears to the amused laughter that rang out behind him. "*Eisey*, David!" shouted Kaptein Pieter. "You must have taken good care of your cattle to have such great herds left to worry about. Mine were all spent long ago!" And even to himself Garib would not admit that it was not only his wealth but also his shame that held him even now that Jonker Afrikaner was dead.

And when two afternoons later Kaptein Pieter suddenly appeared breathless at Garib's hut, Garib was still angry. He tried to shake off the Kaptein's hand as it grabbed his arm.

"David!" panted Kaptein Pieter. "Maherero is gone!"

"Gone?" Garib asked impatiently.

"Yes, gone! While we have been sleeping in the sun he has been taking the cattle under cover of night into the eastern mountains and now he has gone also, and one of his people whom Christian captured says that for some time Maherero has been sending out messages to all the Cattle People, telling them to come to him and already there is a large camp of Black Men guarding the valley where the cattle and sheep are hidden. We have lost everything, David! The Warlike People are nothing but beggars!"

For once there was no gleam in Kaptein Pieter's eyes. He was waving his arms and gibbering like a monkey.

"Why are you wasting time talking?" shouted Garib. "Call the men! Fetch the horses! We must go after Maherero and get back our cattle."

"We cannot!" said Kaptein Pieter. "Maherero has guns now and many men and Christian says they hold the mountain passes!"

Garib stared at him in disbelief. All of Christian Afrikaner's wealth and all of his own wealth which he had built up over the years was disappearing from their sight, and even now the

Warlike People were still going to do nothing.

And suddenly it was more than Garib could bear. He turned his back on Kaptein Pieter, picked up his gun and saddle from the rack on his hut wall and made for the door.

"You cannot go, David!" cried Kaptein Pieter in alarm. "Christian will be angry."

"Christian Afrikaner is not my chief," said Garib. "I am not one of the Warlike People and I will not stay with them longer for I see how it is. They are a low people! They are a people who have lost their courage. They have become nothing but cowards and hyenas. Even Arub the Big One, robber though he has become, has more right to call himself a man than one of you!"

In a fury Garib rushed from the hut. He leapt on to his horse and, using his switch to the utmost, galloped wildly through the searing heat of the afternoon until the beast, its flanks streaming and heaving, and the foam flying from its mouth, stumbled with exhaustion and could run no more.

Garib climbed down from the horse and, still trembling with fury, strained his eyes for a glimpse of Maherero on the plain ahead. But the brown and sunburnt veld was empty, the mountains in the east grey in the fading light of late afternoon. Garib knew that he could not reach them on foot and his horse was too spent to go further.

And as he stood there his anger turned slowly to despair for he knew that even if he could reach Maherero's camp there was nothing he could do to get back the stolen cattle. What could one man achieve against a hundred guns? He would never get through the pass alive or have so much as a glimpse of the flocks and herds in the valley beyond.

Weary and scorched from the heat, Garib led his horse towards the green line of trees which marked the path of a river. Following the dry sandy bed, he came to a small pool which still remained under an overhang of rock.

When he and the horse had drunk their fill, Garib tethered the beast to an overhanging branch and sank down on to the soft warm sand. For a long time he sat without moving and so great was his despair that he did not notice the clouds banking behind him on the eastern horizon or hear the soft ominous roll of distant thunder or see the bright flickers of lightning in the darkening sky.

He was thinking that the missionaries had been right. The kingdoms of evil were utterly destroyed. There was nothing left of all the great kingdom which Jonker Afrikaner had built up. Haramub himself was gone and Ai-gams which had once been so splendid was now like a village which had been overrun by wild dogs and the Warlike People were nothing but beggars.

And sitting there Garib thought about himself also. He did not need the missionaries or Tomarib to tell him that he too had done wrong. He had known it within himself all along. If this were not so would he have felt such shame? And he thought that the Men of God had been right again when they had said there was only one God. There was one wisdom which all men shared. All peoples had a knowledge of good and of evil and knew within themselves how a man should behave. *Ai!* he had indeed done wrong, and now, because of his insults to the Warlike People he had at last cut himself off from them and neither wealth nor position was left to him. He too was little more than a beggar.

And because he no longer cared what might happen, he did what Fast Foot had taught him that no hunter should ever do in the season of storms. He lay down in the dry river bed and went to sleep and he did not even feel the first large splashing drops of rain.

The flood hit Garib at dawn while he was still sleeping. A wall of water almost his own height came thundering down the dry river bed and, with a deafening roar, it tumbled and boiled round the bend of the river and was upon him. Garib was sucked up into its irresistible fury, rolled over and over by the foaming, pounding strength of the flood.

In the first terrible moment of waking Garib could not understand where he was. Then as a branch of an uprooted tree swept past and rolled him down again into the dark muddy torrent, he realized what had happened. There must have been a storm to the east nearer the source of the river. How often had he not experienced these storms when the heavens themselves seemed to open as the rain poured down so that within a short space of time the whole sun-scorched countryside became one shining sheet of water, and waves would roll down the river beds and go on rolling, uprooting all that stood in their way, even beyond the area of the storm, until they had spent their force and had been absorbed into the parched soil.

Garib gasped for air. He struggled and kicked. He was swirled round and round in the torrent, tossed like a straw amid the sticks and branches and other rubbish picked up by the flood. All his life it seemed he had been waiting for this wall of water, waiting fearfully on the bank, unsure of his strength, with the great river of life about to sweep him up into its terrible flood. Now it had happened and he was indeed destroyed.

In the pale light he saw yet another great branch bearing down on him. A mass of wet leaves caught him in the face. He choked and gasped. In a frenzy he struck out with his hands. His arms went round the thick rough trunk. He felt himself being dragged along at a great speed in the foaming torrent, then suddenly the tree gave a lurch and stuck fast against a tangle of debris in the next bend in the river. Bushes, leaves and branches began to pile up, with the water raging behind them. In a moment the trunk would be dislodged again by the weight pushing against it and then all would be lost.

Then Garib saw the other branch above his head. It was the branch of a tree overhanging the river. He grasped at it with one hand, then with the other. It bowed under his weight until it came right down, and with a desperate effort he dragged himself clear of the water and fell exhausted on to the bank.

Garib did not know how long he lay there, but when he opened his eyes again the sun was already rising. He pulled himself into a sitting position, and with a feeling of wonder he touched his face and his arms and slid his hands down the legs of his torn trousers.

"*Eisey!* I am still alive!" he whispered though he could hardly believe that this was true. He stood up slowly and found that he was not only alive but, apart from being stiff and bruised from the battering the flood had given him, unhurt.

Garib looked down at the river. Already the great torrent had spent its force. The stream had shrunk to a murmuring trickle and he knew that even that would soon be gone, leaving the bed dry once more.

Then, remembering his horse which he had tethered higher up the river, he made his way along the bank. He found the broken thong hanging from the tree beside the place where he had been sleeping. In fright at the thundering water the beast must have snapped it and bolted. Quickly Garib ran to the top of the slight rise. There was no sign of the horse. Neither, when he returned and searched up and down the stream, could he find any sign of his gun.

Despair threatened to engulf him once more. His cattle were gone and now his horse and gun had disappeared. He had no more wealth than a small child. Then Garib was aware of a strange lightness. It was as if now that the last of the possessions he had earned as a result of Haramub's raiding had gone, the burden of shame had been lifted from him and he was free.

Free! And suddenly Garib realized that he owed no more allegiance to the Warlike People and he was free to go home. This was what he had wanted for a long time.

Feeling weak and dizzy, Garib sat down on a nearby rock. He thought of his mother and wondered about his younger sister, and then he remembered the pots and the kettle and other trinkets he still had in his hut at Okahandja and he could imagine their pleasure at such gifts which he had earned through his early work of courage in breaking in the ride oxen. *Ai*, he thought not all his life with Haramub had been filled with shame!

Uncertainly, but with the beginning of eagerness, he thought ahead, exploring in his mind the possibilities of returning home. His family was at Hoachanas and Hoachanas was now a mission station. If he returned he would have to do once more as the Men of God demanded and he knew it would not be easy. They were difficult men and they did not understand the Nama people.

But even as he considered the hard path ahead, he thought again of those words which had come back to him in the empty church in Ai-gams, and though he could not recall it all so perfectly, he remembered some of it. "The wolf shall dwell with the lamb.... They shall not hurt nor destroy in all my holy mountain ..."

Garib had come to know, through his experience of life, how when he hurt others, he too was hurt, and how hatred also turned back upon the hater. As a face looked back at itself in a pool of water, so the actions of men reflected back on to themselves. If a man felt such hatred that he wished to kill and destroy, he must surely destroy himself at last also, and, strange as it seemed, Garib could understand that if a man could love his neighbour as the Men of God demanded, he would indeed have fullness of life.

And, though it still seemed impossible to him that enemies could live together in peace, the words seemed like some splendid vision, and in the same instant he knew without doubt, as if in answer to a prayer, that a man must follow the path of good for this was what his own wisdom told him. Along this road lay the glory.

"*Ai!*" Garib whispered in wonder. "The glory!"

Then, standing up, he gazed across the plain in the direction of Christian Afrikaner's camp. It was a long, long way and if he did not wish to starve he must forget about visions and think rather of practical matters. But as he stared apprehensively across the veld he remembered that other terrible walk across the Land of Sand and Stone at the time of the great drought. That had been much further and he had only been a child, yet he had survived.

"I am still Garib Arub even though I am also David," he said to give himself courage. "What I did as a child I can surely do easily now that I am a man." And for the first time, it seemed to Garib, he felt with certainty that he was indeed a man. And more than this, he was a man still in his full strength who might even, through his work, find pride in his manhood.

There would be work for him at Hoachanas. And *eisey!*

What a fool he was to have forgotten! He must hurry for there was a trader waiting at Okahandja for drovers to help him drive his bartered cattle first to Ai-gams, then to Hoachanas.

Quickly Garib set off across the plain and the further he went, the quicker he walked for the air was cool and tingling against his skin and all around the land looked fresh and smiling after the rain. Already, Garib saw with surprise, there was a haze of green showing through the dead dry grass and the soil, which had been rock hard, was moist and springy under his feet as if new life were swelling and thrusting its way up through it. It was always like this after the rain. Soon the veld would be transformed with greenness.

And now Garib understood the meaning of what Tomarib had tried to teach him. "As I die and am renewed, so shall you die and be renewed." This was what the Moon had said. Garib had learnt too much at the mission school to believe that the moon had actually spoken, but he knew at last what the people in their ancient wisdom had been trying to say. While a man lived he should not cease to hope for God was Lord of the World and, if he chose to act with courage as a man, every end might also be a new beginning.

And then Garib was running. Leaping over bushes and shrubs that stood in his way, he ran, as eager as a boy, as swiftly as a hunter, across the great plain and into the new day.